MUSHROOM THEORY

PT BATEMAN

MUSHROOM THEORY

PT BATEMAN

For more information, or to book an event, contact :
info@ptbateman.com
http://www.PTBateman.com

Scan QR to visit Author site
and learn more about upcoming
books and events!

Book Cover design and Layout by Captured by KC Designs
www.capturedbykcdesigns.com

Hardcover: 979-8-9886281-0-1
Paperback: 979-8-9886281-1-8

*To Worth, whose poetry and gentle soul
inspired my muse to speak.*

CHAPTER ONE

Dawson Crane had no idea that he was about to become an expendable pawn in a game of chess where the kings didn't care how many pieces fell, as long as they were the last ones standing. He was emotionally drained as he pulled his Forrester into the well-lit driveway. It had been a long, grueling week at work. He sat behind the steering wheel, staring off into space, absently listening to some old 70's song on the radio. He reflected numbly on the events of the past week.

His research on a new chemical agent had come under scrutiny from his boss and the investors. They had pulled all his work documents and brought them into a large conference room used specifically for research discovery. Everything had been laid out and each page was read, under what felt like the proverbial microscope. The investors painstakingly scrutinized every test, every analysis, every hypothesis, and every conclusion. These weren't the company's ordinary, interested-party investors either. They were the kind of investors that wanted things in a neat and orderly fashion, and they wanted every detail accurate. This particular group of investors were the Pentagon's very own chemical warfare advisors. They were looking for answers, and a scapegoat. Their sights were laser-focused on Dawson.

The war in Ukraine had uncovered the use of a mysterious chemical the Russians were using on civilians and the United States government wanted to know how the agent came about and what they could do, or use, to stop it. It was Dawson's assignment to find what the agent was and how to counteract it. They wanted answers. They wanted the answers now. His bosses, and the investors, weren't the only ones interested in Dawson's research.

Dawson first learned about the chemical agent from what looked to be, an anonymous email he received a couple of weeks ago. When the email alert had sounded on his computer, the software previewed part of the message, showing just a few sentences of the body of the text. At first, he thought the email was spam and was ready to hit the delete button when two words caught his eye and he paused with his index finger hovering over delete. The words were, *unimaginable horror.* A simple phrase that spurs images of panic and dread even though the phrase itself contradicts the process. He glanced at the sender's name: Akoval@ bobblemail.ur. Dawson immediately opened the email to reveal the entire text, curious as to why Andriy would be using his personal email account.

Andriy Koval, a friend and Ukrainian soldier, laid out in his email the atrocities of the Ukrainian/Russian war. The US news outlets covered the story telling the American people in simple, sensationalist terms, Russia had invaded Ukraine under false pretenses, bombed their cities regardless of civilian occupancy, and captured and tortured Ukrainian soldiers violating the rules of the Geneva Convention. The American public was outraged at the audacity of another country, especially Russia, bullying, much less invading, a smaller, peaceful nation. Money from Congress was sent, fundraisers were started to help with the food shortages, and weapons were flown in to help in the fight. With the US and other NATO nations' help, it looked like Ukraine was not only standing its' ground but pushing the invading forces back. It felt like Deja-vu of what happened ten years prior. Until this.

Andriy elaborated in his email. Civilians were being found dead in the streets covered in pustules. The soldiers were afraid to move the bodies, so they left them there for the news outlets to converge and cover the footage. At first, the public thought the conditions of the bodies were simply a product of the bombs and missiles. *Burn blisters* was the term they used. Nothing else was said about it, or investigated further, so the news crews had moved on. But there was more to these mis-named burn blisters than just the heat of missile attacks.

As most soldiers, Andriy had been mandated by the Ukrainian government, as a capable male of fighting age. His occupation before the war broke out was that of a biochemical engineer. His work specialized in the use of chemical warfare. He hadn't expected to put his knowledge to use during this war. At least, he hoped he wouldn't have to, but having seen what happened in Syria years before, he wasn't too surprised his skills would be needed. What he was seeing on the bodies of the dead civilians in the streets was not simply burns from previously used chemicals, this was much more sinister.

Andriy had been patrolling a small town at dusk when he first came across bodies inflicted with these blisters. Carefully, he approached a man lying in the debris just outside of a recently bombed out building. Smoke still billowed where the bomb had hit the second floor of what used to be a library. The stench of smoke, concrete dust, and burnt flesh hung stagnantly in the air. The man must have been searching for a book to read to pass the time of war thinking it would never reach his small town. Little did he know his fingers would never touch the spine of an interesting publication.

Everything around Andriy looked gray. The once lush, manicured gardens and landscape now lay powdered in ash and dust, like Pompeii after the eruption of Mount Vesuvius. Pages and pages of books still scattered in the breeze, blowing the once bound works of literature like flower petals up in the air and across the debris filled streets.

Andriy stepped closer to the man. He quickly looked around to see if any Russian soldiers were nearby. He didn't want to be captured. He didn't want to get shot. Most of all, he didn't want to be killed. Upon inspection, the man looked to be about 30 years old. It was hard to tell the exact age as he was covered in ash and dust like everything else. The man lay face down in the ruins. His arms were pressed against his side, but his legs were sprawled out in a position that wasn't natural for the human body. Blood had pooled around the man's head. The blood was fresh but not fresh enough to still be red. It had darkened from being exposed to the air and now was a putrid, dark brown, almost black blanket spread around his head.

Carefully, Andriy turned the man over, using his boot. He didn't like handling a fellow countryman this way, but he didn't want to touch the cold, stiffness of the man. He saw something glint around the man's neck. Andriy thought it was a necklace. He hesitantly reached for the man's collar. He didn't want to leave anything of value for the Russian soldiers to take. As he carefully pulled back the tattered, blood and soot-stained shirt, he gasped, recoiling at what he saw. A patch of blisters about a fist's width in diameter was embedded at the base of the man's neck. The canker was huge, about an inch round and a half inch tall. He immediately thought this was the use of chemical warfare although he had never seen this type of wound pattern before. The pustules were filled with a brownish tint to the fluid looking as if they would burst any second. That, in itself, was unique as the body naturally fills a blister with a clear serum to help cushion the affected area and combat any potential infection.

Andriy quickly scrambled to pull out a basic medical pack all soldiers had been given as part of their military gear. He found a small scalpel whose main purpose was to help dig out any bullets a soldier may get shot with. He also found a couple small zip lock bags whose intended use was to gather those bullets for forensic evidence against the Russians. He hoped the bags were leak proof.

He picked up the scalpel in his shaking hand and leaned over the man, ready to prick the bubble when he suddenly stopped. He had forgotten to put on gloves. He needed to calm down before he made a bigger mistake.

Andriy sat back on his heels as he pulled out his medical bag again and found a pair of latex surgical gloves. His pulse was racing, and his hands were sweaty. The gloves didn't pull on to his hands easily. He took his time. Pulling on the gloves slowly over each finger before finally his palm and wrist. He didn't need the gloves to rip. He had no idea when medical supplies would be replenished, and his supplies were running low.

Once prepped for the task at hand, Andriy ever so gently scraped some skin around the blister and put the sample into one zip lock bag and sealed it. He grabbed another bag and opened it. He placed the opened flap of the bag directly under one of the larger blisters. Using the tip of the scalpel, he pricked a small hole at the base of the bubbled skin. A thick, brownish colored fluid slowly oozed out the blister causing Andriy to hold back the urge to gag. He didn't want to push on the blister causing it to explode in a rush of ooze, but he didn't want to stay where he was much longer either. Taking the scalpel, he cut the hole a fraction longer so the fluid would flow a little faster. He didn't realize he was holding his breath, and as the last of the fluid was collected, he let it out slowly. He stood up, looked around again, and started to leave. He stopped short and looked back at the man lying there. Andriy moved back to the body, bowed his head, and said a small prayer for the man's soul before he turned again and walked away.

Not far from where the man laid, a woman's body was sprawled, face up, in the street. Andriy quickly ran to her and examined her neck. She had on a sleeveless, scoop-neck dress, and even though it was cold outside, she wasn't wearing a coat. He speculated that maybe she too had been inside the library when it exploded. Upon closer inspection, Andriy noticed she had the abnormal fist-shaped blister cluster at the base of her neck, close to her throat, like the man he had just examined. He reached again for his medical pack when he heard gunfire in the distance. He didn't want to wait around to see if it was going to get closer. He stood up and hurriedly moved away from the body. He needed to get to a lab to find out what he had just uncovered. He had a long journey ahead of him. The Lutsk Lab was the closest lab, but it was over ten miles away, deep in Russian occupied territory. Adding to his dilemma, Andriy didn't have any way to get there except for his own two feet. Any vehicle he could possibly acquire would be either stopped and checked or blown to bits immediately. Quietly, deftly, he quickly walked out of the small town, heading towards the lab, passing the once well-kept yards. He didn't notice the brown mushrooms lurking in the ash covered lawns.

A commercial for fast food fries blasted across the radio bringing Dawson out of his trance. *Why do commercials always seem louder than the music on the same channel?* Dawson thought to himself.

He turned off the ignition, picked up his laptop bag, and got out of the car. He pushed the lock button on the key fob. The ever annoying – *beep, beep*, told him that the doors were locked and the auto alarm set.

As Dawson walked along his walkway to the house, he noticed the lawn. The grass had grown in leaps and bounds due to the recent warm, sunny days and spring showers. He knew tomorrow was going to be *lawn day*, as his small cul-de-sac neighbors fondly called it. Lawn days were Saturdays during the Spring and Summer months where the neighbors showed off their lawn maintenance skills to boast who had the best-looking lawn. Bragging rights were given to the yard with the most meticulously kept lawn and it was a friendly competition with a small sliver of arrogance. Dawson hung his head as he shuffled towards the house. He never got bragging rights.

CHAPTER TWO

"Well, I'm not going to win any awards with this lawn," Dawson mumbled under his breath staring at his front lawn, as he sipped his morning coffee. He had come out to the front porch to survey his yard. The day was sunny, warm enough to break a sweat if you were directly in the sun, with a soft, adequate breeze fluttering the flags hanging on their poles. His grass wasn't any taller than his neighbors, as they all tended to mow their lawns on the same day every week. There weren't any dandelions or other weeds growing either. There were, however, mushrooms. Big mushrooms. Sometimes, if the weather was muggy at night yet cool, mushrooms seemed to spring up overnight.

Dawson was familiar with that phenomenon. It appeared to have been what happened here, yet these mushrooms weren't anything Dawson had seen before; however, given the ever-changing climate due to global warming, nothing surprised him anymore where the weather was concerned. The usual mushrooms he encountered were tiny white, half-closed umbrella shaped mushrooms that usually died off in a day or two of hot weather. These invaders were brown and the size of softballs yet only with a slightly rounded top. Perplexed, Dawson stared at them from the distance of the porch as he finished off his coffee. After a moment, he turned and went back inside the house.

Dawson rinsed out his coffee cup and placed it inside the dishwasher. Closing the door, he heard the distant hum of a lawn mower. Turning towards the sound, he realized Tom had started mowing his lawn. Tom was always the first to start lawn day. Tom was a bit of a recluse. Dawson had only spoken with him at the cul-de-sac cookouts they would have once or twice a year during the summer, depending on the weather.

From what Dawson remembered of the few, short conversations he had had with him, Tom Bosman was a writer. Dawson had never heard of him so maybe he wasn't a very good writer. That or he used a pen name he didn't care to share when discussing their respective jobs with each other. Tom, however, won most of the lawn day bragging rights.

Tom's lawn belonged to the first house upon entering the cul-de-sac. There were only five houses total on the cul-de-sac and each lawn was an acre of land with about 200 feet of front footage with the houses situated more towards the front of the plot rather than the back. Thuja Green Giant lined the border of Tom's house with that of his neighbor, Alex Sharp. Alex was hardly ever home; he had moved into the neighborhood not too long after ChemComm had taken a research contract for the Pentagon last spring. Dawson remembered trying to pry Alex for his line of work, but he always avoided the subject.

The Thuja stood about 18-feet tall and made a natural fence line that helped enhance Tom's seclusion. Each house was a cookie cutter colonial with white composite wrap-around front porches and a two-car garage. No house was more than 2,600 square feet and no less than 2,400 square feet. All had four bedrooms with two and a half baths. The main difference in the square footage was that two of the houses had a three-season sun room attached to the back of the house and the others did not. The only discernible difference between the outside front of the houses were their colors. Tom's house was a soft beige with burgundy shutters, Alex's was a pale blue with darker blue shutters. Dawson was happy with his light gray siding and black shutters. The other two houses were variants of the same colors: blue with maroon shutters, and beige with black shutters.

HOA guidelines kept homeowners from attempting to go rogue and have anything outside of what was considered appropriate curb appeal.

The front of Tom's house was flanked by pristine flower beds the width of the front porch. The two rectangular shaped beds were parted by a flagstone sidewalk consisting of varying sizes and tones of beige that wound its way to the driveway from the front porch steps. Tom's flowerbeds consisted of pink knockout azaleas and vibrant green boxwood. The bushes were trimmed to perfection without a single branch or flower daring to protrude out of place. As boring as it would seem to appear, the topography had a certain order of beauty about it.

Dawson shut the dishwasher door and headed upstairs to change out of his sleeping clothes. *Time to get this done, he* thought as he climbed the stairs. He put on a pair of olive-green khaki shorts and an oversized white t-shirt. This was his lawn day outfit. He chuckled to himself as he dressed, thinking how utterly mundane his life was outside of work. *Work.* He didn't want to think about the week he had. He immediately pushed down the thoughts of the government advisors scrutinizing his research and glaring at him with such menace in their eyes because he hadn't found the solution to their problem. He took the stairs two at a time, eventually making his way through the kitchen. He bounded through the door to the garage, determined to win lawn day.

Stepping inside the spacious garage, pungent smells of grass, paint, and cardboard filled his nostrils. The garage was a mess with boxes marked *Stephanie* strewn about. Dawson's ex-girlfriend was a bit of a pack-rat and it had taken Dawson about a month to gather all her belongings and box them up. A bit of sadness fell over him as he looked at the boxes.

Stephanie and Dawson had been together for about two years when she decided to end their relationship and fly off to Poland on some sort of genealogical lineage search for her ancestors. Her friends and distant cousins had encouraged her to go, and it didn't take much persuasion for her to do so. She felt, as she told Dawson about the decision, their relationship wasn't heading in the direction she had hoped it would. The announcement had come out of the blue and took Dawson by surprise. Thinking back, he realized he had ignored the signs.

The month before her abrupt departure had been the worst. He had been coming home from work tired and not engaging much in conversation for weeks. It eventually took a toll on their relationship. He couldn't imagine how things would have been given his latest assignment. He was working even longer hours than he had before. They didn't eat dinner together, didn't have date nights or even time for the intimacy all couples need to share in order to maintain that deeper connection in a relationship.

The project he had been assigned to had him working 15-hour days, six days a week. He was forbidden to talk to Stephanie about the project as it was deemed highly classified. She was an adventurous spirit and that's what had attracted Dawson to her in the first place. She needed to be on the go all the time. She couldn't see herself grounded to a man whose job anchored him to one place.

Stephanie had asked Dawson to pack up her belongings and she would send for them once she settled, for the time being, in Poland. *Poland.* The thought of where she was currently residing greatly concerned him even if she was among friends. She was very much near the war and very much near danger. Pushing the dreaded thoughts deeper into his subconscious, Dawson maneuvered himself around the boxes until he reached the lawnmower.

CHAPTER THREE

The route to Andriy's lab wasn't as smooth as he had hoped. The first night of his journey had been tricky. Navigating the war-torn terrain precariously close to where the Russians were continuing their bombings of cities and homes, proved to be almost impossible. Keeping close to the rubble of the destroyed buildings he found was his best chance of survival. Buildings that weren't even five years old, demolished again from the onslaught of the war. Buildings his fellow countrymen and women had stepped up to rebuild after the occupation was overthrown a decade ago. Buildings where life had once returned along with never ending hope encapsulated in the souls of the Ukrainian people.

Occasionally, he would hear the Russian soldiers' gunfire in the distance but closer than he would have liked. Sounds similar to fireworks from the celebrations the country had held after fighting off the Russians. But these weren't fireworks, and this definitely wasn't a celebration in the distance. He had to keep moving. Their gunfire seemed haphazard as if they were not shooting at any target in particular, simply firing off rounds of ammo for fun. Andriy would soon realize that the shooting was indeed precise, and the targets were civilians.

One night, searching to find somewhere to get some much-needed sleep, he came upon a building that appeared to have been destroyed weeks ago. From its outward appearance, it had previously been a small apartment building only three stories tall. It had housed maybe twelve different families who either escaped when the shelling started, or they lay dead and buried underneath the rubble. The third and second floors of dwellings had fallen onto the first floor, splitting its ceiling in half. Furniture, appliances, clothes, and other various personal belongings lay scattered inside and out of the place once home to its occupants. Steel bars and broken concrete formed open pockets of small spaces. Andriy decided to take advantage of the impromptu cover.

He had been traveling during the night to avoid being seen during the day. He had only progressed four miles in two days' time. The distance didn't seem very far to have been covered in that time frame but trying to avoid any encounters with the soldiers had demonstrated the need for utter cat-like agility and caution. It was an exhaustive trip especially factoring in the pure fight or flight adrenaline coursing through his body constantly. He needed safety to alleviate his nerves even if it was just temporary or false optimism. He needed to think. He needed a plan. Most of all, he just wanted to rest. Hunkering down into the tiny space, he relaxed his muscles and his thoughts. Slowly, sleep took hold.

He was abruptly awoken by the sounds of bullets ricocheting off the concrete rubble very close to his makeshift shelter. The high-pitched whistle and immediate impact of a bullet six inches from his head quickly brought him out of his slumber. Chaotic sounds broke the imaginary sense of serenity in which he had been resting. Reality has a way of waking one up very fast. He heard loud, shrill screams of pure fear. Screams of men and women that were instantaneously silenced. Footsteps pounding the pavement of those frantically trying to outrun the gunman's bullets, but they weren't fast enough. He could hear the Russians shouting at people to stop, deceivingly stating they meant no harm. He heard footsteps abruptly stop running, hoping that what the soldiers were saying would be true. Andriy envisioned them turning towards their enemy, begging for mercy. He knew they would fall to their knees, hands clenched together outstretched towards the soldiers; tears streaming down their faces, pleading for their lives. The forgiveness granted was in the form of a five-millimeter hole in the center of their heads to those who willingly surrendered. The men and women fell where they knelt. Their apathetic killers simply moved on after their targets lay motionless. The soldiers' voices were getting closer. Their steady, purposeful walk was very near to where he had taken refuge. Andriy ever so quietly crouched further under the rubble trying to make himself invisible. He didn't breathe. He didn't move a muscle. The only indication he was still alive was his eyes rapidly flicking left and right looking for soldiers and the perspiration that slid down his face. He wondered if the soldiers could smell his sweat the same way predators seek their prey.

"Prodolzyhay dvigat'sya. Keep moving." One soldier yelled, causing him to jolt at the booming voice so close to him. Others called out again for citizens to surrender. Summoning them to their deaths.

Andriy heard a few more rounds of bullets fired sporadically as the soldiers moved on through the town, gunning down those they encountered as they forged ahead. The bullets ricocheted off the ruins or just randomly shot in the air. The sheer arrogance of the soldiers could not be mistaken. After about ten minutes without hearing gunfire, his body ever so slowly began to stop shaking and he carefully started to move out of the shelter. He peeked over the rubble surveying the area, keenly watching for any sudden movement. Ready to retreat at any second. He saw the bodies of those who foolishly tried to surrender and the bodies of those who foolishly tried to escape. Stepping over the broken ruins, his foot caught a piece of shattered concrete sending several bits tumbling down around him.

Instantly, he froze and covered his head. Pure fear wracked his body. He knew the soldiers must have heard the noise, praying that they did not. The sound was amplified inside the hollowness of the building.

Andriy closed his eyes tightly shut as if he could not bear to look at the bullet that promised to be on its way to his head. But nothing came. Just silence. The only source of sound was that of his rapidly beating heart echoing in his ears.

Andriy guardedly opened his eyes. Frantically, patting himself down, he let out a sigh of relief that his body was still in one piece. He was still on this Earth, still in this hellhole. He wasn't sure why he was relieved, but he was. The afterlife would be much better than where he was now, but for some reason, his purpose needed to continue here. His right hand felt the two small packages he carried in his right pant pocket. He pulled the packets out checking to make sure the contents were still intact and hadn't leaked in all his scrambling around jagged fragments. The brownish fluid was still there, swirling in its container. Nothing had escaped. Pushing the packets back into his pocket, he picked his way through the fallen bodies stopping only briefly to, again, pray for their souls and continued his journey to the lab.

CHAPTER FOUR

Dawson opened the garage door and pushed the riding mower out onto the driveway. More mowers could be heard throughout the cul-de-sac, and he knew he was falling behind in the lawn day race. He bought the red Troy-Bilt mower used through some local online marketplace he had stumbled upon. He paid $250 for the mower, and it ran beautifully. Dawson's paltry analyst salary couldn't spare the money the other neighbors laid out for their high-priced mowers. Dawson chuckled at the thought of the sweet deal he got and still was able to save face. *How vain even men are sometimes*, he thought.

Dawson started with the front lawn, mowing close to the porch first. He spotted the mushrooms again, but they were clustered closer to the road than the front of the house. *I'll get to them last*, he reasoned and continued his ride.

His mind numbed from the sound of the mower cutting through the blades of grass. His thoughts turned to the email he had received from Andriy and how they had met; it seemed like an eternity ago. He recalled his first encounter with Andriy at a chemical engineering convention last year. Dawson couldn't fathom why his company would send him to London to attend this international event. Maybe they thought more of him than he gave them credit for.

At the conference, he had just finished listening to a particularly boring round of speakers droning on and on about chemical reactions, commercial chemical uses, chemical solvency, and chemical antidotes. Yawning, Dawson exited the conference auditorium and headed for the hotel bar. After ordering a glass of straight bourbon, a boyish-faced man sat down next to him. From the looks of him, he had been just as weary from the topic of today's discussion as he had.

"Hey, there," Dawson said, offering his hand. "I take it you found the lecture rather dull too."

"Yes. I am not understanding why I am even here." Taking Dawson's hand and shaking it. The man's accent was familiar, but Dawson didn't want to be rude and assume anything.

"I know what you mean. I'm Dawson Crane from ChemComm Corporation in Belfast, Maine. In the United States, not Ireland", he added with a smile, introducing himself.

"Andriy Koval." The man replied, extending his hand to Dawson. "My company, Lutsk Laboratories, sent me here hoping to learn information for how to produce larger crop yields for our country."

"Oh, yeah? What country are you from?" Dawson inquired, sipping his bourbon.

"Ukraine. Our country is the largest exporter of wheat, but we are running out of land to use so we need to find a way to make our crops produce more in the ever-shrinking land space," he explained.

"Why are you here?" Andriy queried.

"Oh, you know. The corporate suits decided to send the analysts to gather the information to bring back to the company. That way, they could get the details without having to sit through all the monotonous industry jargon," Dawson said.

Andriy had a perplexed look on his face, so Dawson tried again. "They didn't want to sit through boring lectures, so they sent me instead," he explained half-jokingly. Andriy nodded his head in understanding.

Andriy ordered a vodka, neat. He and Dawson continued their

conversation about chemicals, each gathering tidbits of information about each other along the way. Dawson wished he could talk to Stephanie like he was with Andriy. There's something about conversing with another person who completely understands what you are saying and is interested in the topic as well. Stephanie never took an interest in chemistry. Stephanie never took an interest in anything that was as complicated and cumbersome as science subjects were for her. Those topics completely went against her free-spirited nature. She wanted to talk about travel, Hinduism, and the language of bees. Chemical engineering just wasn't in her vocabulary.

Dawson learned that Andriy's company was located about 400KM west of Kyiv, Ukraine's capital city, in Lutsk. The company had been started just after the installation of President Zelensky's successor, Borysko Bagan. Bagan's election win elated the Ukrainians. Zelensky had taken Ukraine through the conflict ten years ago and rebuilt most of the country. It was a long, arduous process, but the country was gradually bouncing back, except for the wheat crops.

About two years into the conflict, there was a coup that ousted the Russian president. Military leaders seized control of the country and while they decided to end the conflict with their bordering country, it was just a matter of time before the new regime wanted to try its hand again at taking back what they thought was theirs.

Tensions between the two countries had been building for years. President Bagan wanted to ensure Ukraine's place on the world stage and its wheat crop was the ticket for its continued admittance. He also wanted to fortify his new allegiance with NATO and the other willing countries that had helped his predecessor before the coup. He started Lutsk Laboratories in an attempt to increase the yield of the country's precious wheat crops. Ukraine's population was exploding with more and more people relocating to the comparatively small nation. More people meant less viable crop land. He needed to find a way to produce more with less. The lab he had commissioned was starting to make headway in its search for farming chemicals to bolster crops when another global pandemic hit. As with most companies, work stopped. The lab's research also came to a complete halt.

When the worst of it was over and with the gradual reopening of businesses spreading across the globe, Lutsk Laboratories started reinvesting in its research. The escalating tensions with the Russian regime under the dictatorship of General Nicholi Gorsky were reaching a boiling point, and they needed to hurriedly find a solution to the crop problem before there were no crops to worry about. Getting the land to produce more and then exported was paramount to the survival of Ukraine's economy. A symposium of chemical engineers was being held in London for analysts to gather information from other nations facing similar circumstances. The rest of the world was wrestling with urbanization reducing the available agriculture land, and they were seeking the same answers as Ukraine; how to do more with less? How to keep crops producing in the rising temperatures and chaotic weather patterns? It seemed to be a worldwide theme. This was also the chance for the lab to gain additional knowledge to speed up and boost production.

Andriy's company chose him to attend the conference as he was their brightest, most qualified analyst. Andriy had studied chemical engineering at the University of Surrey in England, not very far from where the symposium was being held. He graduated in the top two percent of his class with a master's degree in biochemical engineering and a bachelor's degree in botany before returning to Ukraine. With his degrees, he was immediately tapped for the newly established lab straight out of the university.

Dawson was duly impressed with Andriy's background and education. Dawson held a master's degree in biochemical engineering as well, but he only minored in human physiology as an afterthought. The studies in human physiology were just to entertain himself. He had lost his spleen in a skateboard accident when he was twelve. In his research, he learned that the spleen helps filter alcohol for the liver.

Without a spleen, Dawson got drunk more rapidly than his friends. They called him a lightweight. He just thought he was saving money not having to buy that much alcohol at the college keg parties, as everyone contributed towards the purchase of the kegs. Not having a spleen also made him more susceptible to infections, so he was placed on a regimen of bland foods and plenty of fluids. Dawson considered beer a type of fluid substitute.

Not having a spleen also made Dawson defenseless to a rare autoimmune disease. He remembered the hospital, the doctor's grim looks, the tests, and the agonizing trials to find a cure. Dawson had started feeling ill during his junior year at UMaine Hutchinson. He simply attributed it to too many beer challenges during Friday Frat nights. He was far off the mark. His spleen removal had finally caught up with him and triggered the rare autoimmune disease his doctor's had warned him about a decade ago.

Test after test was conducted. Dawson got progressively worse. His weight dropped considerably. Nothing stayed down. The doctors put him on a feeding tube to nourish his body and organs. So many blood samples were taken that he began to think he was in a secret lab designed for subversive vampires. All the tests came back the same. An autoimmune disease without a name. A disease without a cure. A patient without a chance of survival.

Dawson had undergone so many tests without results, he felt himself giving up. He thought about ending it all and saving everyone, including himself, the embarrassment of failure. If a cure couldn't be found soon, Dawson wouldn't have to worry about living much longer anyway. He didn't realize that some doctors in the medical profession took these kinds of cases as a challenge. They were revitalized by the notion that something existed that couldn't be explained by science. In hidden egotism, they were looking for the glory of being the one who discovered an unknown disease, and its cure, so their names would be emblazoned on some hospital wing on the East Coast.

An up-and-coming scientist by the name of Dr. Davio Stenner was called in to advise the doctors on Dawson's case. Stenner had been researching obscure autoimmune diseases. One particularly rare diagnosis, called autoimmune hepatitis, was what Dr. Stenner had been exploring. His journal articles were discovered by one of the doctors assigned to Dawson's case. His most recent white papers uncovered Stenner's experiments using mycelium, a type of fungus found in the common mushroom.

His test patients, rats, were experiencing the same symptoms as Dawson and the results of the research found a possible cure. However, there was no true correlation between the mycelium spores and the remedy for the disease. More research was needed before any federal agency would approve its use on humans. The doctors were grasping at straws trying to save Dawson. Stenner's work was their only foreseeable hope. They entered Dawson's room with a proposal. He agreed. Stenner flew into town the next day.

Dawson quickly squelched the memories of the treatment that ensued under Dr. Stenner's direction, returning his focus to the lawn.

CHAPTER FIVE

Closing in on the last row of the front lawn, Dawson started the lawn mower and stared at the patch of grass where the mushrooms had clustered. Glancing towards his neighbor's yard, he noticed Bob Calvert perched on his riding mower staring intently at the ground in front of him. Bob lived in the blue house, maroon shuttered colonial. Bob was a bit of a bad comedian that told dad jokes, especially when it came to his own name.

At the cul-de-sac parties, he'd walk up to Dawson or Alex or Tom and ask, "What do you call something floating in the pool? Bob," he'd say, clapping the back of the poor listener, rolling in his own laughter.

Tom would politely walk away muttering, "That's a good one, Bob." Alex always tried to counter with a vulgar joke. Bob never thought those were funny.

Bob had stopped about ten feet in front of a cluster of mushrooms. From what Dawson could see, they were the same shape and size as the ones in his yard. He looked around at the other yards, and in each yard, he noticed identical patches of the brown fungi. He couldn't see all the way into Tom's yard due to his self-installed green barrier, but he surmised that his lawn contained the same clusters given the weather conditions over the last few days. At least, that's what Dawson chalked their presence up to.

Bob glanced over at Dawson and raised his arm in recognition of his attendance on lawn day. Bob was shirtless; a practice he should have given up about ten years and twenty pounds ago. Dawson nodded and waved back. Bob then lowered his arms, hands grasping the steering wheel, his back-end slightly raised as if he were participating in a 50-yard dash. With a devilish and somewhat childish yell, Bob spurred his mower towards the ghastly nuisance. As he ran over the mushrooms, a large blast of brown smoke-like dust rushed from underneath the mower. Dawson stared amused at Bob's laughter in his triumph over the fungal invaders.

With his own mower approaching the cluster, Dawson too decided to have a little fun at their destruction and mimicked Bob's yell. He had the same results of brown smoke spewing from the obliteration point. He stopped his mower and watched as the cloud expanded along the ground before gently rising and dispersing in the air. He looked back to where they had been growing and noticed that the stems of the mushrooms were still intact. He put the mower in neutral and hopped off to investigate. Using the tip of his tennis shoe, he kicked the stem. It wiggled like flexible rubber and didn't break apart upon impact. Intrigued, Dawson stooped down for a closer inspection.

Tiny holes pocketed the stem making it look more like a sponge. Dawson reached out to touch it. It was cool and dry. Not brittle dry, but not moist either. He stood up and stomped on the stem. When he looked again, the stem had not altered its appearance. It simply bounced back into its former shape. He turned to look at Bob trying to see if he had had a similar experience. Putting one hand up over his eyes to block the sun, he glanced in Bob's direction. Bob wasn't there.

Dawson saw Bob's mower and could hear it still running although stationary at the moment. *Bob must have stopped to look at his accomplishment,* Dawson surmised. His eyes searched the yard. Dawson's arm dropped to his side as the dreaded realization crept into vision. Bob was lying face down in the yard. The lawn mower partially concealed his lower torso. He looked as if he had been trying to get into the house because he had fallen close to the front porch steps. Dawson hurriedly shut off the lawn mower and ran across the cul-de-sac to Bob's lawn.

As Dawson got closer, he could see Bob's arms and legs twitching sporadically. Bob's head was turned on its side, looking in the direction where Dawson had previously been on his mower.

"Bob?! Are you alright?" Dawson frantically yelled as he approached. The twitching started to worsen.

Bob didn't answer. His stare was pointed, not moving towards the sound of Dawson's voice. The convulsions made Bob's arms and legs flail about like a fish desperately trying to get back into water before the air killed it. Yellowish-brown foam started oozing out from Bob's parted lips. He looked as if he was in the middle of a cry for help but was silenced before the words could be heard.

Dawson reached for his phone to call 9-1-1. It wasn't in his pocket. He had left it in the house on the charger because he had been so distracted last night, he had forgotten to charge it.

"I'll be right back." He told Bob, as he turned towards his own house. In his panic, he almost blurted out, "Don't move."

He rushed across the street. Taking the three steps to his porch in one jump, he bolted through the front door. He saw his phone lying on the kitchen counter. He quickly picked up the phone and dialed the emergency number.

"9-1-1. What's your emergency?" The dispatcher asked in a practiced monotone voice.

"Help. My neighbor. Something's wrong." Dawson managed to say shakingly into the phone.

"Sir. I need you to calm down." She responded.

"What?" Dawson asked incredulously to the dispatcher. "I can't calm down. My neighbor is lying face down in his yard and he's foaming at the mouth like some rapid dog! Please send help. Now!"

"Sir. Tell me your address so I can send responders to the scene." Her voice evenly conveyed her request.

Dawson took a deep breath. He was still shaking, and his thoughts were rapidly racing through his head, but he managed to tell the dispatcher his address and where Bob lived. Hanging up, he swiftly ran back outside and over to Bob's house. Approaching Bob again, Dawson noticed he wasn't twitching anymore. His eyes were still fixed but the stare was empty. The bubbly foam gathered around Bob's mouth, not flowing anymore. His face was frozen; contoured in fear. Dawson let out a defeated sigh, closing his eyes as the death of his neighbor sank in.

Dawson walked away from Bob, towards his house and sat down on Bob's front porch steps. He silently waited for the paramedics to arrive. He held his head in his hands as he rested his elbows on his knees. He rocked gently back and forth trying to figure out what had happened. He replayed the scenes in his head searching for logic. He couldn't find any. After about a minute, but what seemed like an eternity, Dawson heard the shrieking sounds of sirens rapidly approaching their location. *Too late*, he thought.

Dawson looked up at the now diminished sounds from the ambulance and firetruck making their way down the street towards their cul-de-sac. Something caught his eye as he had raised his head. There was something strange in the middle of Bob's back. From where he sat, he could see where a cluster of dark blisters had formed. Dawson started to get up for a closer look when the paramedics rushed to where Bob was lying, preventing Dawson from approaching further.

"Can you tell us what happened here, sir?", the medic asked, holding his arm out to Dawson, keeping him in his place. The man was wearing a navy-blue uniform that fit him like a glove. He looked like a model for one of those fireman beefcake calendars they sell for fundraisers for the firehouse station. His name tag said Henderson. Henderson looked to be in his early to mid-20's, fresh out of the academy. His sandy blonde hair brightened by the sun.

"I'm not sure." Dawson replied, unable to think of what could have happened other than Bob innocently mowing his lawn on a beautiful Saturday morning. "He had just started mowing his lawn, as I had, and then when I glanced over, he wasn't on his lawn mower anymore."

Other emergency personnel arrived on the scene and started performing CPR on Bob. When they turned him over, Dawson noticed more clusters of blisters on Bob's chest. Three groups of blisters, all the same size as the one on his back formed on his skin. One grouping, in particular, was gathered at the base of his neck. All had large blisters filled with a brownish looking fluid. Something sparked in Dawson's memory. Andriy's email. *But how? How did what Andriy described happening to the civilians in the Russian-Ukrainian war manifest itself here?* It had to be a coincidence.

What Andriy had been describing was chemical warfare. The US wasn't a part of the situation except for sending aid and some clandestine military weapons to assist the Ukrainians in their efforts to stop the invasion as they had done in the past war. The covert reasoning for the backing of the Ukrainian government was to secure the wheat. The US had made a backdoor deal with Ukraine after the last war to help bolster its economy by becoming a major wheat importer, and had, over time, become quite dependent on its crops. Everyone knew it but no one dared speak about it. The US wasn't about to allow its people to starve, let alone the entire world. Even South America and Africa sent some sort of aid to help secure their investments in the crops.

Dawson paced around the yard trying to find the connection. General Gorsky wouldn't be so bold as to start a war with the United States. He had nuclear weapons, sure, but he flaunted them as if he were a silverback gorilla, pounding its chest in dominance. It was all for show because he knew if he used them, his entire country would be obliterated in a matter of minutes. But then, so would the rest of the world. It was a scenario that would never play out and Gorsky knew it.

Henderson walked over to Dawson, who had sat back down on Bob's front steps, while the medical personnel did what they needed to.

"Sir, do you know if the gentleman had any relatives?" He asked.

Had. He said had. *Past tense.* Bob was dead.

Dawson knew it before the paramedics arrived, but the words nailed in the obvious. "No, he didn't. His wife passed away about two years ago. It was just him." Dawson sighed.

"We're going to need some identification of the victim for our records. He didn't seem to have any on him. Maybe he left his wallet in his house. Do you have access to his house?"

"Bob. His name is...*was* Bob. Bob Calvert." Dawson said, a little confrontational.

"I'm sorry for your loss. Was he a friend?" Henderson asked sympathetically.

"More of an acquaintance. You know, a neighbor you say 'Hi' to in passing or have a generic conversation with now and then." Dawson said. "Nothing substantial." He added.

"Are you able to explain what may have caused this?" Henderson asked again now that Dawson appeared more composed than when he first inquired about the situation.

Dawson explained about the mushrooms and the effect running over them with a lawn mower caused. Henderson listened, jotting down notes, not really intrigued by what had transpired. He just needed the information for his paperwork and for the standard questions the medical examiner would ask after he brought the body to the hospital's morgue. He left out any reference to his emails with Andriy and what they had contained. He wasn't even sure the two incidents were connected, but he felt it best not to divulge any unnecessary details. Henderson and the other emergency personnel wrapped Bob's body in a dark green tarp and placed him on the stretcher. They wheeled him to the ambulance, hoisted him inside and closed the doors. Dawson watched as the units pulled away from the front of Bob's house and started to leave the cul-de-sac.

"Stop!" Dawson shouted suddenly. Dawson heard the firetruck brake. The equipment had been blocking his view of Tom's house. Once cleared, he saw Tom. He too was lying face down on the ground next to his steps. "There's another body." Dawson pointing, his voice trembling.

CHAPTER SIX

Andriy paused. He had been clandestinely traveling for a few days. They all seemed to have blended together. Between hiding from the Russian soldiers, holding up in bombed out buildings for minutes of rest at a time, and scavenging for food and water, he was exhausted. He estimated that he was a mile from the lab.

Just ten minutes, he thought. *Just give me ten minutes to rest.*

He came upon another broken building. They all looked alike now. Structures half stood with their interiors exposed to the elements. Metal and concrete precariously hanging from its host. Office supplies from businesses, dining room tables from houses, food from restaurants and toys from children all littered the streets. Occasionally, there was total obliteration; contents buried beneath an unrecognizable establishment without any sense of what once was previously conducted within its walls.

Carefully entering the demolished building, he searched for a place to hide. Listening again for any outside sounds that would send him scrambling for sanctuary, he gradually moved further into the abyss. Plopping down within the confines of the rubble, a small puff of gray ash swirled around Andriy. He didn't care. He just wanted to rest. He was filthy, hungry, thirsty, and most of all tired. He knew he needed to get to the lab.

He wasn't quite sure what he was going to do once he got there, so he started laying out a plan in his head.

First, he needed to find out what the fluid inside the blisters consisted of. Having never seen this before, he wasn't certain he had the resources to ascertain its properties. His research was mainly improving wheat production, not blisters on dead people. He couldn't recall, in any of his university studies, such a case either. He wasn't even sure whom to ask to help him identify it. His colleagues were fighting the war too, not that they would have been much help. Most of them had just recently graduated from the university only majoring in general science. Since general science consisted of a requirement of three chemistry classes, they were hired by Lutsk Laboratories as entry level analysts. Time was running out finding the solution to the dwindling wheat supplies and the corporate leaders needed anyone with even an ounce of chemical knowledge.

Suddenly, he remembered the conference he attended last year in London. He had been sent by the lab to try and gain any information that may be useful in their task. Scientific speakers from around the world talked about everything except how to bolster food yield. Some touched on genetically modified organisms, or GMO as it was commonly termed. Ukraine had been using GMO for years and although the wheat grains were bigger, it didn't solve the shrinking land problem. He came away from the week-long conference with nothing more than what he came with.

He tried to recall the man he spoke with after an extraordinarily boring presentation. He had gone to the hotel bar and found him sitting there. He recognized him from the session he had just left. Sitting down, the man introduced himself.

What was his name? Andriy tried to recall. He remembered he said he was from Belfast. When he said where he was from, Andriy recalled immediately questioning the man in his head because his accent did not match that of someone from Belfast. Then he continued with the geographical location of the United States. Maine was the state he mentioned. At least that's what he thought he recalled.

Belfast, Maine. Yes, that was right. That's what stuck in his head. *But what was his name?* Andriy's eyes grew heavy, and his thoughts started fading to the point where he couldn't concentrate any longer. His body succumbed to sleep.

Something touched his shoulder. Andriy jumped from his slumber, hoisted his rifle in front of him and took aim. A frightened child stood wide-eyed and scared in front of him, not moving a muscle. He must have been looking for a place to hide away from the soldiers as Andriy had. Andriy must also have been in such a deep sleep he didn't hear the boy until he was right upon him. He didn't like that his defenses had been shut down.

"Slava Ukraini." The boy whispered hesitantly.

"Slava Ukraini." Andriy repeated as he relaxed his shoulders, and lowered the gun.

"What are you doing here?" He asked the obviously scared boy.

He also wondered how the boy found him so deeply hidden in the rubble. He wasn't too keen on the thought that he hadn't heard the boy approaching either. He'd have to either hide better next time or take shorter naps. Andriy sat down again and patted a spot next to him, inviting the boy to sit down. He didn't want to frighten the boy, but the adrenaline rush he had just experienced still lingered in his voice.

"My mama and papa are dead. They were killed by the Russian soldiers yesterday." He started. "I was at primary school when they came into town. My school was bombed and many of us were hurt. Some died," he said, sadly. "The soldiers started shooting everywhere. I hid until I didn't hear them anymore. When I went home, my mama and papa were in the living room, watching TV, waiting for me to come home. They were shot in the head. The soldiers took our food and left. Do you have anything to eat?" He suddenly asked as if his stomach reminded him of his hunger.

Andriy's heart ached listening to this small child so matter-of-factly telling him of the horrors he had witnessed less than 24 hours before. The trauma had voided him of any emotions. He guessed the boy to be about nine years old. He had curly brown hair speckled with dust and ash that seemed everywhere. His brown leather shoes looked new as if purchased for the beginning of the school year but obviously still too big for his feet that weren't growing as fast as he was. He was wearing a long-sleeved, white shirt. Well, it was originally white until he found himself outside in the elements for the past day. His black pants hung loosely on his hips, his parents would have hoped that this pair would last more than six months, and he could gradually grow into them. He stood about four foot high and had the telltale high pitched voice of males who hadn't reached puberty. His eyes were somber and sad, but he wasn't crying.

At the mention of food, Andriy's stomach growled too. He couldn't remember the last time he had eaten. He stood up and beckoned the boy to follow him.

"I think I saw a small market not too far away. Let's see if the soldiers left any food." He said, trying to sound positive.

The boy's eyes lit up at the reference to food and readily followed Andriy out of the shelter, into the streets.

The two walked about a block before they came upon what used to be a farmer's market of some sort. Most towns had these markets where the locals could purchase what they needed for each meal rather than buy an entire week's worth of food at the grocery store a few miles away. There wasn't much produce left. The Russian soldiers had been hungry too. They found two apples and a dust crusted block of cheese. Andriy brushed off the dirt as best he could and broke the block in half, handing one piece to the boy. The boy hurriedly grabbed the cheese, dust and all and then bit into one of the apples. He had closed his eyes as he ate, savoring the sweet fruit with contentment.

Andriy and the boy stood there as they ate the food. Both were a little more relaxed now that their stomachs, though not nearly full enough, were at least not growling any longer.

"What is your name?" Andriy inquired.

"Fedir." The boy replied.

Fedir meant *gift from God*. Andriy could see why his parents had chosen the name. Fedir looked angelic as most children do at that age.

Andriy and Fedir finished their meal and stepped back into the streets. Instinct made Andriy inspect their surroundings. Finding nothing menacing, they continued their walk. He weighed the pros and cons of taking him with him to the lab. Andriy couldn't see leaving the boy here by himself. *How would he survive?*

There wasn't anything really to decide. The boy either had to come with him or he had to find out if he had any family in the surrounding area that he could take him to.

He turned to Fedir. "Do you have any family nearby?" He asked.

"No. My aunts left to go to Poland when the war started and took my cousins. My uncles stayed behind to help fight. I haven't seen them since they left." He simply stated.

"Would you like to come with me? I'm trying to get to the place where I work. We should be safe there until I can find a way to leave the country." Andriy explained.

Fedir smiled up at him and nodded his head in excitement and relief. Andriy grinned back at the boy, as they began walking together back towards the lab.

CHAPTER SEVEN

"Tom!" Dawson yelled. He raced across the cul-de-sac to Tom's yard. The paramedics had stopped and exited their vehicle. They were not far behind Dawson. Tom lay just as Bob had, face down in the yard. The mower was still running, so Dawson ran over and turned it off. Luckily, the mower's safety features kicked in as soon as Tom's foot left the gas pedal. From the looks of him, he had been trying to get inside. His body lay close to his front steps. The sun had started to burn his legs where his shorts ended, and his arms were turning pink as well. He must have fallen about the same time Bob had, but Dawson had been concentrating on Bob and was unaware.

The paramedics turned Tom over on to his back and started resuscitation measures. Dawson heard the one, two, three, breathe exercise as they tried to revive Tom. His eyes were closed. The measures didn't seem to be working. Dawson stepped over to where the efforts were being made but maintained a safe distance. He didn't want to be reprimanded again for being too close. The paramedics had torn open Tom's shirt to attempt defibrillation. Immediately, Dawson noticed the blister clusters. *What could be causing this?* He questioned to himself.

Running his hand through his hair, Dawson stared at Tom. Then, looking around the yard, he could see that Tom had almost finished mowing the front lawn. His mower lines were pristine. The flower beds contained more plants than Bob's did, but they weren't in bad taste or overrun with them. He had filled the beds with purple irises, and they were getting ready to bloom. A few more warm days and the entire bed would be a royal robe of purple. Dawson spotted the brown, spongy bottoms of the mushrooms. His mind was racing. *Could this possibly be what Andriy had spoken about in his email?* He couldn't think that there could be any correlation. He needed to review the email again. *Chemical warfare? Here? It just couldn't be.* There had to be another explanation.

He heard the paramedics shouting, "Clear!" His thoughts turned back to Tom. He just looked at him in wonder. The blisters, the brownish liquid; exactly the same as Bob's. Exactly the same as Andriy had explained it. *How could this be?* His mind screamed! He wanted to bolt from the place and get to his computer, but he didn't want to alarm the medics.

He stayed there until the paramedics loaded the zipped, black body bag. Numbly, he answered their questions about Tom. How long did he know him? How long had he lived in his house? Did he have any next of kin? Their questions seemed to come in rapid fire succession. Dawson answered them as best he could. He didn't know if Tom had any relatives. The topic never came up in the cul-de-sac parties. He just assumed he had a family. He knew he wasn't married, but that was about all he knew. He watched the ambulance and fire trucks drive away. The other two houses stood vacant. Alex was out of town. He would need to get a hold of him and warn him to stay away. The grass needed to be mowed and Dawson knew a lawn service would be there soon. He would need to warn the lawn company too, wondering what he could possibly say that wouldn't sound outrageous. He started to cross the cul-de-sac to examine the lawns but stopped when he remembered the email was much more important. He headed towards his house; his mind disoriented by all the information flooding it.

As he walked through the door, the weight of all he just witnessed came crashing down on his thoughts. He slumped down in a chair in the living room. *Bob and Tom were dead!* His mind could not fathom all he had seen in a relatively short time. *Dead! From what?* He wondered.

Springing up from his chair, he walked over to his desk and opened the laptop. He searched his emails looking for the one from Andriy. At first, he couldn't locate it. It wasn't still in his inbox. He looked to the left of the screen to his saved folders and found the one labeled confidential. He clicked on the folder icon. There it was. Dated March 22, 2032. *Could it have only been a month ago?*

He read the email again. Andriy had laid out a description of what he had seen in the streets of the bombed-out cities he traversed in Ukraine. He detailed the two bodies he found with curious blister clusters. He had gathered tissue samples and the fluids contained within the blisters. He had reached his lab in less than a week. It had been a long and grueling, if not emotional, journey before he had been able to reach the lab. Dawson read about how Andriy had needed to hide from the Russian soldiers and the boy he brought with him to the lab after discovering his parents killed.

He told Dawson of his gruesome findings. The fluid contained Zyclon B. A chemical the Nazi's had used on the Jewish detainees in the concentration camps during World War II. Something that was outlawed at the end of the war. He also discovered myceloids. Mushroom spores. The two together formed a rare, illegal chemical called Zyklonmycolodide, or ZMD for short. From what Andriy speculated, the Russians were injecting mushrooms with Zyclon B. Any time the mushroom was destroyed, the spores would be emitted into the air. He believed these spores caused death within five minutes of contact. Andriy concluded in his email that he needed further research. He didn't remember seeing any mushrooms along his journey but admitted his mind had been on more pressing matters. He wasn't sure how much longer he could investigate given the circumstances and the war. He would reach out to Dawson when and if he found out more. And if he could possibly find an antidote.

Dawson stared at the screen. The meaning of the words slowly sinking into his consciousness. *Chemical warfare.* But how could what Andriy discovered possibly be the same as what Dawson had seen with his neighbors? And how was he not affected? He jumped from the chair, tore off his shirt and raced upstairs to the bathroom mirror. He looked all over his chest and back. No blisters. No sign of any redness or rash. He apparently was not affected by the destruction of the mushrooms. *The mushrooms!*

Dawson raced back downstairs and out the front door. He stopped, turned around and went back into the house. He needed some materials to gather the mushrooms. He went into the cabinet under the sink where he kept a standard medical kit. He rummaged through it and gathered up some gloves and a scalpel. He opened his pantry, retrieved a couple Ziploc sandwich bags, and ran back out of the house.

His senses were on high alert at the possibility of the mushrooms containing ZMD. He felt silly looking around to see if he was being watched, but that's exactly what he did. Cautiously, he approached Tom's house first since it was the closest. Slowly, Dawson walked to where the stem of the mushrooms still stood. He somehow thought the mere tread of his footsteps would set them exploding again. He noticed his heart was racing and he tried to calm his thoughts. Taking a deep breath, he approached the cluster, letting the air out of his lungs. Squatting down next to the grouping with the scalpel in hand, he carefully sliced a piece of the stem off and put it in the bag. He didn't know if he should gather more samples or would this one be enough. Summoning his research knowledge, he decided to cut another piece from a second stem. He stood up and zipped both bags closed. He then turned and walked to Bob's house to do the same. After taking what he needed, he walked back to his house, four samples in hand and thought about what to do next.

Above the cul-de-sac, a small, unnoticeable drone hovered with a camera so powerful it could capture the hairs on a bumblebee from the flowers below. It transmitted the images and data to a remote bunker located in Rycec, Belarus. The analysts reviewing the recordings watched the events unfold below. The tiny, undetectable drone, silently tracking the deaths of the two neighbors, tracking Dawson Crane gathering samples from the mushrooms and tracking the fact that Crane wasn't dead.

CHAPTER EIGHT

Andriy and Fedir finally reached the lab. They had made good time since the Russian soldiers moved on to another city that was not in their path to the lab. Stopping only to rest and eat the scarce food they were able to find, they covered the rest of the journey in five days. They arrived at the lab dirty, covered in grime and sweat. They were thirsty. They were hungry. They were beyond exhausted. They were alive.

The lab was dark not only because it was night outside but also because there wasn't any electricity fed to the building. The power grid that supplied the building had been destroyed by the Russian Air Force in the first days of the war. The strategy was to wipe out all possible energy supplies first so the Ukrainians would eventually surrender. When that didn't work, destruction quickly followed, starting with military bases.

Andriy had not been able to keep his radio on, so he was unsure of the events that had taken place in the last few days. Not only was he trying to conserve the battery, but he was too afraid the sounds would announce his presence to any stray troops along his trek to the lab. Given the reports, the city sounded like it had been untouched by the war. The Russians tried to take over the Capital, but it appeared that the Ukrainian soldiers had been able to keep them out of the Capital, for now. The enemy simply moved around the city and kept going towards other towns, including Lutsk. They were assured by their commanders another offensive would come through and destroy it later as a glorious finale. Andriy breathed a sigh of relief and pride at that knowledge.

He walked over to the secured door and entered his passcode on the keypad. *The lab's backup batteries that kept the locks secured must still be operational*, he thought.

The door opened immediately, and they went inside. Closing the door left them both in total blackness of the windowless entryway. He put his hand on Fedir's chest holding him in place as he fumbled for a flashlight. A split second of doubt crossed his mind. He wondered if it would be safe to use the light, or, if he did, would they both be found out. He had to assume the lab was under Russian control, but he couldn't be sure if they had moved on or not. *Could Gorsky have left a patrol behind?*

He weighed the possibilities in his mind before he decided to click the on button and flood their space with light. He let out a sigh of relief that no gunfire greeted the illumination.

Quietly, they walked the darkened corridors until they reached Andriy's office. He opened his door and quickly shooed Fedir inside, closing the door behind them. Placing the flashlight upright on his desk so to brighten his office space, he sat down at his desk. He motioned Fedir to the small couch by the wall opposite his desk. Ever so slowly he relaxed in his seat. His muscles began to unwind, and his head began to tilt to the side. The last image he saw was Fedir curled in a ball; both falling fast asleep.

About an hour later, he was startled from his slumber. The thoughts of the past days flooded his consciousness and he had awoken with a start. He was sweating again. He listened for any sounds that may have been the culprit for his sudden alertness. Not hearing anything, he started to relax some and realized it was just the dream he had been having that had woken him. He opened his desk drawer where he kept a small stash of food. He had been known to work late nights; well past the time any stores were still open. He kept the food for those occasions. He found some nonperishables including potato chips, peanut butter crackers, chocolate bars, and some chewing gum. Not the most nutritional feast, but it would stave off some of their hunger for now. His tiny dorm sized refrigerator contained small bottles of water. He grabbed two bottles and closed the door.

He debated whether to wake Fedir. The boy looked so peaceful sleeping. Andriy thought about the horrors his young years had shown him. A boy his age should have never been witness to the atrocities of war. No one should witness them. Especially in this day and age. Andriy wasn't necessarily a pacifist, but he never understood why there was such a separation among mankind. We were all made of flesh and blood. We all had the same desires of peace for ourselves and our families.

The human race should be of one race, yet wars had been waged since the dawn of time because someone wanted something different. Someone wanted possession of what someone else had and there was no stopping them from getting it. Years of inventions of destruction made sure of that. *To what end?* Andriy angrily thought. *Until there was nothing left of this Earth? Is that what it would take for annihilation to stop?* He just couldn't wrap his head around the thought.

Continuing to watch Fedir sleep, he reflected on his own youth. He didn't like remembering his past. It was full of heartache. When the first war broke out, he was still in secondary school; too young to be recruited into the forces but old enough to want to. His mother and father were considered middle class. They had enough money to be able to afford the necessities, and occasionally, a small family vacation to Greece. Andriy smiled at that memory. He loved the clear, blue waters surrounding the island. He loved jumping off the cliffs and the exhilaration that came with it. No boy of ten has the fear of mortality in him at that daring, young age.

But the war saw his father leave the house. His mother didn't handle the mandatory recruitment very well. Andriy recalled many occasions waking up in the middle of the night listening to his mother cry into her pillow. The pay from the Army wasn't near what his father's income had been so money became very tight. Several times, he and his mother would only have a biscuit and a piece of fruit for the entire day. With Andriy in his active growing stage, this caused constant hunger pains in the boy. He had tried to put on a brave face for his mother and shrug off his hunger so that she would eat. She rarely would. School was open but quite often the students were sent home when the air raid sirens sounded. On the occasions he was in school, he was fed government-supplied meals. It sustained him some and his belly was full, but he could never be sure when his next meal would be. Sometimes, on his way home from school, he would check the dumpsters for any scraps.

Andriy slowly watched his mother deteriorate from heartache and hunger. He tried to find work, but no one would hire a boy of his age. No one had the money to hire him anyway. His father tried to send money when he could, but the post wasn't running regularly so there wasn't a steady income at home. When some money would arrive, Andriy and his mother still had trouble finding food. Supplies were being held up due to the war and the Russians blocking roads traveling into the cities. What little food they could find was almost triple in price than it was before. The money ran out quickly.

One day, after the air raid sirens sent students and teachers home, Andriy walked home as he normally would. He had a nagging feeling in the pit of his stomach, but he equated it to hunger pains. He was able to get breakfast at the school before the sirens sounded, but his growing body wanted more. Traveling down the street to his parents' house, he noticed his neighbors all gathered in his front yard. From the looks on their faces, he knew something wasn't right. The nagging feeling turned quickly to dread, and he knew it wasn't hunger this time. As he approached his house, the old man that lived next door came up to him and started talking to him to try and distract him from going inside. He was holding Andriy by the shoulders asking him about his day at school and if he was frightened by the sirens. Andriy tried to break the man's grip, but his fingers dug into his shoulders. Finally, he forcefully unlocked himself from the man's hold and bolted into the house past the solemn stares of the others.

A paramedic was blocking his view when he entered the house. He saw his mother slumped in the blue cushioned chair she always sat in while she watched the television. He could see her head turned slightly to the side and her eyes were closed. When the paramedic stood up at the sound of Andriy's entrance, it opened his view to what had been blocked. He could see the blood. A dark, red spot was slightly off-center to the left of her ear and blood flowed down her shirt onto her legs. Andriy was too shocked to speak. The paramedic came over to him and placed his hands on Andriy's shoulder much like the old man in the yard had done except he wasn't as forceful. His voice was calm but assertive as he told Andriy what happened. The reasoning didn't matter. His mother was dead. His father was fighting a war. He was alone.

Andriy shook himself from the memory and looked over at the sleeping boy. He decided to let Fedir sleep. He needed his rest. He needed some sort of break from reality, even if it was only temporary. Andriy needed to get away from his thoughts and the images of that tragic day that still lingered.

He quietly left his office and headed to the laboratory. He made his way to the spectrometer located in the back of the lab. He turned on the switch to the mini compressed air generator. Each mini generator was fed from a larger air tank kept in the basement of the lab and each piece of equipment in the lab was connected to it in case of power outages. The hum of power gradually increased in frequency until it was fully ready for use. His heart raced at the sound, fearing it all could be heard from outside the building.

Trying to calm himself he turned on the spectrometer and it quickly came to life. Carefully retrieving the two samples in his pocket, he opened the bag containing the fluid first. Grabbing a dropper, he sucked up a small amount of fluid and placed it on a slide. He put the slide in the machine and waited for the results. While waiting, he prepared another slide of the tissue he had scrapped from the dead man in the street. A memory of the man flashed in Andriy's mind, and he silently said another prayer while waiting for the machine to reveal its outcome.

The results of the first sampling were ready, indicated by a tiny chime from the machine. Andriy stared in disbelief at the sequence of compounds. *It couldn't be.*

He had only seen this particular chemical sequence in his historical warfare studies at the university. But this wasn't a history class. This was now. To ensure that the results were accurate, he ran the test again. He shakily prepared another slide and waited with bated breath for the results again. The same conclusion printed out on the paper. Zyclon B. It was the demonic chemical the Third Reich had used on the innocent Jewish people in the concentration camps scattered throughout Germany during World War II. *This can't be real*, he thought.

All of Germany agreed to destroy it after 2008 when people started realizing that it was still in production. Andriy slammed his fist on the counter, bouncing the machine and the slides from their resting place. He was angered at the thought that someone hid the chemical. *Someone purposely hid this deadly, catastrophic chemical for future use!*

Quickly, he ran the sample of the skin tissue. At the chime of the spectrometer, he studied its results. There was Zyclon B and another substance. Myceloids. Mushroom spores.

Why would Zyclon B and mushroom spores be in the blisters of a dead man's body? What was the connection? He pondered to himself.

As Andriy put two and two together, he knew he had to tell someone his findings. *Crane! Dawson Crane!* His name popped into Andriy's head as he sprinted down the hall to his office. Quietly entering the room, he sat down at his desk and opened his laptop. He had shut down the computer before he left for the war. He wasn't sure it had enough battery life in it, but he turned it on to find out. The light from the screen illuminated Andriy's face as he searched for the battery life icon. Finding it, he noticed he only had seven percent power left. He searched around for the power cord until he realized he had lent it to a coworker the last time he was at the lab. He had forgotten to get it back before he had left for the day. The next day, he was mandated into the war.

He composed an email to Crane using the hot-spot on his phone to connect to the internet. He outlined what he had witnessed, what he had gathered, and what his results were. He also sent the email from his personal email account that he could switch to from his laptop's email program. He didn't want to have the lab's email exchange out there in cyberspace for who knew who to notice. *You are being paranoid.* Andriy thought. *No,* he countered himself, *I'm being cautious.*

Within minutes he received an acknowledgment from Dawson. It seemed an impersonal response – *Got it.* Andriy stared at the words trying to decipher any meaning when his phone suddenly lit up with a red circle.

"Shit! A virus!" He frantically tried to turn off his phone and laptop, but he was too late. Both screens went black.

At a bunker not far from Andriy's lab, Sergei Breskov's computer sounded an alarm. He had been mindlessly playing a new version of the latest cyber war video game when the alarm came through. It was triggered by an email message containing the words Zyclon B. Sergei sat up straight in his chair. He wasn't sure what to do. He was hired only to monitor the computer for any unusual activity.

For the past three months, he noticed nothing unusual. In fact, this was the best job he could have landed for his twenty-year-old self. A full-time job that basically paid him to play video games nine hours a day with lunch always provided by the company. The palms of his hands were instantly sweating in panic.

After tracing the IP address of the sender's laptop, he pushed the button to disable the device and its hot-spot. He then picked up his phone, dialing the private phone number he had been given for instances such as this. He had read about it in the handbook he was given on his first day on the job.

"We have a situation." He said into the phone as it was answered. His supervisor listened to his reading of the emailed message. He was thanked for the information and abruptly rewarded with a click of disconnection. The supervisor called the investor. He was not pleased with what was just relayed to him. A third call was made. This time to an undisclosed phone number with a Washington D.C. area code.

CHAPTER NINE

Stephanie Blevins loved Poland. She had only been there a week and had already fallen in love with the people and the places. The sights delighted her carefree nature. Her desire to research her ancestry had brought her here. Her breakup with Dawson had pushed her to fulfill that desire. She loved Dawson but his work hours and non-commitment to a more wholesome partnership left her feeling the need to leave. She had hoped he would change. She had tried to introduce him to a less stressful life. She found local parks to take him to try and engage him in nature. She took him to art museums to encourage him to contemplate each stroke of the artist's brush. She even tried aroma therapy, placing incense throughout the house filling the rooms with smells of lavender and chamomile. Nothing seemed to work. Dawson was just too intrigued with his work. The long hours took a toll on their relationship until she had enough. When she left, she only took the essentials for her trip. She needed to write to Dawson to have her stuff sent but she kept putting it off. She could get by with what she brought with her.

Her friends welcomed her with open arms when she deboarded the plane. Her arrival took their minds off the war that had just started. Their parents had spoken of the *time before*. They were children when the first war had broken out and as time went on and the war had ended, the bitterness had faded. Now, they anticipated this war would end like the last and everything would return to normal. There wasn't a need to panic in their minds.

They met Stephanie at the airport and took her to their home where they had prepared a room for her. The room was lovely. They filled it with the local flowers and a bedspread that was hand quilted by a village woman. The scent of the throw smelled of jasmine perfume and Stephanie wrapped herself in calming vapors. She was very tired from all the plane rides it took to get here, and her friends understood the need for some rest before a true visit could begin.

The day after her arrival, she started the research of her family's ancestors. Her friend, Cara, took her to the local library. Cara embraced the distraction from the war and eagerly embarked with her American friend. Stephanie and Cara hadn't seen each other since college but she wrote to Cara often about her journey to find her past. The architecture of the building was stunning. The two-story white edifice stood with beaming white columns holding the white stone awning of the entrance. Granite sculptures adorned each side of the massive mahogany double doors. To one side was a sculpture of the Polish chronicler, soldier, and priest Jan Długosz and Polish educationalist, Hugo Kołłątaj. Both men were contributors to the history of Poland and to the library. Their statues alone gave Stephanie the impression that the library would be able to unearth the stories she longed to read about her ancestors.

She spent the next two weeks combing over volumes of marriage records, birth records and the unseeming mountainous amounts of death records. She wrote pages and pages of notes about the ancestors she uncovered. There wasn't much about relatives long passed due to the decimation of the Polish libraries during the second World War, but she was able to find information about her great grandparents, cousins that had died in the concentration camps, those that were liberated, aunts that had started their own business, and uncles that had lived through the

Warsaw Ghetto uprising. She soaked in all that she could find. There were a few times she wanted to call Dawson to tell him about the facts she had discovered in her research. He would love the details she had been able to unravel and piece back together to tell her own history. She sighed when she thought about him, longing to hear his voice again, but she pushed the memories aside and pressed on with her studies.

The downside to her arrival was the almost sudden outbreak of war in Ukraine. The threat of war had been circulating for about a week before she had arrived, but the people had brushed off the idea of another invasion in less than a decade. But it did happen again. This time, the Russian military was in control. Stephanie feared this time would be much, much worse. From what she had uncovered about her own ancestors and their struggles with military dictators, she didn't think the Ukrainians would push back the invaders as smartly and quickly as they did last time.

There was talk that refugees would start coming to the Polish border within the next week or two. Her friends wanted to be at the front lines to support the influx of women and children as much as possible. She initially didn't want to be involved but the concern her friends showed told her it was time to put aside her research for now and join the cause. They started gathering supplies to fill whatever vehicles were available in order to drive to the border to help set up triage sites and camps.

Stephanie helped in the effort by picking up supplies where she could. She drove to villages accepting whatever food they were willing to supply. She drove to pharmacies to gather medical supplies. Gloves, bandages, antibiotic creams and pills were obtained and added to the piles. Aid was coming in from all over the world, but more would be needed. She tracked down a bottling company and was given cases of water to take. After about a week of preparation, Stephanie and her friends headed to the border. It would be a two-day trip.

They arrived at the border to instant organized chaos. The influx was more overwhelming than anyone had anticipated but everyone quickly adapted as if the war a decade ago prepared them for similar conditions that they had found themselves faced with again. Stephanie and her friends were separated to where they were needed most. Stephanie was assigned to assist in the medical tents since it was her vehicle that contained the most medical supplies. No one asked her if she had any sort of medical background. It really didn't matter. She went where she was told.

At first, the refugees were well kept citizens simply fleeing their country for, what they thought would be, a short stay. Women and children of all ages crossed the border passing the yellow and black poles that were lifted to let them in. They were neat and clean as if they were crossing the border to vacation in the neighboring countryside rather than fleeing an invasion. They wore fine clothes; some even wore jewelry around their necks. There were no security checks, no one to tell them to stop. They just flowed into the safety of the welcoming parties that guided them to various tents for food or supplies or just a place to rest for a bit. Some carried small suitcases or simple plastic trash bags filled only with clothes and personal items small enough not to be a burden on their long walk. Children wore backpacks with their belongings relying on their mothers to carry the rest of the load. They were scared by the bombs, but they weren't injured. Their husbands, boyfriends and even sons were not among the groups entering the country. They had stayed behind whether by mandatory orders or just the desire to defend their country again.

Stephanie quickly learned that most of the people spoke Polish. She tried her best from what she had learned of the language when she was little. She brokenly conversed with mothers scared about what would happen with their sons. They had left their homes, their jobs, their very lifestyle. The sorrow was short lived as they also spoke about what would happen, according to them, in about a month's time. She listened to the women saying they thought that they would be returning home very soon. They expected the newly formed civilian soldiers would push the Russians back to where they came from. Pride beamed in their faces when they spoke about how brave the Ukrainian men were. Nothing would overcome their pride. Not even General Gorsky and his much more sophisticated army.

They had been through this before and, even though the coup stopped the last invasion, they knew they had the willingness to overcome this one too.

The women were sent to various areas of need, much of them not needing more than a place to sleep and something to eat. They would chat with the other women that crossed the border. The common theme was the missing of their men. The young wives were much calmer than the mothers who had lived through this before. The wives and girlfriends would reassure one another, saying that their men would turn back the Russian military in quick time and they would all reunite in no time. The older women were not as optimistic as their younger counterparts.

As the days went on, the clothes on the incoming refugees became more tattered looking. There weren't as many suitcases as in the beginning. The distance traveled was longer or more dangerous. Cars and other transportation had been either stolen by the Russians or blown up in their attacks, so the crowds, coming in on foot were dirty from the journey. The need for essentials was increasing and the supplies were decreasing. The atmosphere filled with dread and fear replacing the once hopeful tone. More and more were coming across the border injured requiring medical attention. Some were carried, so malnourished from the journey, they died before they were able to get any food, despite everyone's efforts to save them. Things were looking grim, but Stephanie could not tear herself away. If anything, she felt more compelled to help.

She started working more closely with the medical staff. At first, she simply dressed the minor cuts and bruises. She gave water to those who had become dehydrated along the way. Then, as time elapsed, she was called to assist in more dire conditions. She stitched gashes and cuts. She removed shrapnel embedded in young arms and legs. She tended to the torn skin of the feet of the children from walking such a long distance. Occasionally, a rare military train would arrive full of wounded soldiers. She did her best to triage the men into categories of serious injuries.

The smell was overwhelming. Blood, sweat, and urine filled her nostrils. Sometimes it was so overpowering she had to excuse herself from the tents to vomit. Still, she stayed. She couldn't leave. They needed her. She and the others were their family now. There were a few men among the refugees; those too weak or broken to fight. Brothers were not sure where the other was or even if they were alive since they were fit enough to fight. Fathers too old to fight searched for their injured sons. Some were reunited, some were not. Mothers could be heard crying as she walked through the sea of makeshift tents that seemed to go on for miles.

One day, Stephanie was aiding in a medical tent filled with soldiers with a most peculiar rash. Their chests were covered in tiny, brown blisters. The nurses wiped the blisters with rubbing alcohol and that seemed to alleviate some of the itching sensations the soldiers complained about. With supplies dwindling, the best they could do was clean them, smear them with some antibiotic ointment and put a gauze pad over them.

Not too long after the men were treated, the nurses started to get sick. At first, they were nauseous. They left the tents to walk around the back and empty the contents of their stomachs. They would return and continue to treat the men. Stephanie watched as, one by one, the nurses stepped outside only to return a few minutes later and press on. Stephanie didn't minister to the much more seriously wounded. Her job was to gather and give the needed medication and supplies to the nurses and to tend to minor cuts and scrapes. Still, she felt that she needed to get out of the tent. One nurse collapsed in the middle of dressing one soldier's wounds. She jumped up and headed towards the tent next door where the doctors were performing more serious procedures for the more serious wounds.

"Help!" She called out. A young female doctor stopped attending to a soldier she had been trying to remove a bullet from. "What is it?" She asked.

"The nurses." Stephanie stammered. "They're all getting sick!"

"Tell them to get some fresh air." She replied and turned back to her patient.

Fresh air isn't going to do any good, Stephanie thought to herself. She turned back towards the medical tent just as her stomach began to churn and she found herself behind the tents with the others.

CHAPTER TEN

Harold Tomlin couldn't concentrate on the meeting. He desperately wanted to attend to the phone message waiting for him, but his absence would be noted. Two weeks ago, he had had a phone call from the same number as the one listed as leaving him a message this time. He was to be contacted through the phone number in cases of emergencies only. He wasn't pleased with that call, and he doubted he'd be pleased with this one either. He was vaguely listening to the Pentagon officials and people from ChemComm apprise every one of the research results that had been uncovered. A chemical engineer by the name of Dawson Crane was working on a theory that the Russian regime could possibly be using chemical warfare.

Two intense weeks of research was plastered on the projection screen for all to see. The officials and lab rats were up in arms at the thought of this. They spoke of the atrocities that were being recorded on civilian phones and posted on social media pages. If the American people found out that ChemComm knew what was happening and didn't sound the alarm, the company would be shut down immediately. ChemComm had a duty to uncover this violation, if it were true, and find an antidote to help the Ukrainian people.

The men continued to talk rapidly in disbelief of the findings. There had to be a mistake. The Russians wouldn't break Geneva Convention edicts. What would be General Gorsky's motive? If we find the antidote, at least three of them would get Nobel prizes. Everyone seemed to be talking at once. Tomlin knew all this, but he feigned interest and outrage along with everyone else. He knew of Crane research, he knew of Andriy's email that triggered his research, and he knew things were starting to unravel. He had planned to have Crane and his research eliminated, but somehow, he just knew that the message waiting for him would reveal the task had not been carried out. Tomlin was a pessimist because in his line of work, optimism never prevailed.

"I will get to the bottom of this," he sternly told them; his brow furrowed in feigned anger. "I will use all the Pentagon resources at my disposal. I will contact all the necessary United States' agencies and start an internal investigation." No stone would be left unturned, he assured them. Tomlin was a formidable man with an authoritative voice. His words instantly pacified them and the meeting adjourned. Tomlin hastily left.

Slightly reclining in the driver's seat of his black Suburban, free of any listening devices, he pulled out his phone and tapped the message icon.

"He's still alive." The message simply said. Tomlin's anger started to rise. He erased the message and using his secure phone, dialed the phone number, seething as he waited for it to be picked up.

"Privyet." The male voice answered in Russian.

"What happened?" Tomlin snarled into the phone. "I thought you said you could take care of him."

"He wasn't affected by the agent," the male voice stated.

"How could that be?" Tomlin asked incredulously.

"I don't know." Was the simple reply.

"Look, I took a risk on this plan of yours. You said you could take care of him. You assured me you could take care of them both! Now Crane is still alive and so is Koval. You've had an entire month to eliminate them. A month! Koval is traveling with a boy, for Christ's sake, and you still haven't found him." Tomlin practically shouted into the phone.

"I couldn't risk being exposed. I also had to wait for the temperature to start to rise before I could plant the mushrooms," the male voice, unaffected by Tomlin's outburst, explained.

"I wasn't crazy about this plan in the first place. The whole idea risked the entire operation. The two labs are working together, it's not going to take them very long to put the pieces together," Tomlin countered.

"I'll take care of it. I'll deal with Crane first and then I can eliminate Koval," the caller calmly assured him.

"What about the neighbors? I've seen the drone footage. You do realize that an autopsy will be performed on them both? Another exposure risk you've put me in." Tomlin quipped.

"I'll have my people intercept the medical examiner's computer and his notes. It'll look like they both died from natural causes and the whole thing was a freak act of nature. The Americans are so gullible; they'll believe it. Don't worry. I'll handle the cleanup," he said decisively.

"You better!", Tomlin warned. "And take care of the girl while you're at it. She's a potential liability. My gut tells me Crane will get in contact with her, and I don't want any loose ends.", he added abruptly hanging up the phone.

The caller disconnected and tapped the screen connected to his center console. Crane was still home according to the drone footage. He put the car in drive and headed towards Belfast's city limits. Knowing Tomlin would not be happy with the news he had just relayed, he had taken the first flight to Maine. He had just arrived in Maine when Tomlin called.

During the drive from the airport, he thought about how he would eliminate Crane. With the neighbors gone, it would be some time before anyone would realize he was dead. He could stage the house to make it look like a robbery gone bad. He could make his death look like a suicide. Everyone knew he was still whining over losing his girlfriend. Hell, he could even make it look like a mowing accident and have Crane found trapped under his mower. He chuckled. *It would serve him right*, the man thought.

The road to the quiet cul-de-sac would take the man about an hour. He was calm in his thoughts. Killing someone never bothered him. It was almost therapeutic. It was what he had been trained from an early age to do. He knew how to shoot a gun by the time he was seven years old. He knew how to kill someone by the time he was ten. In fact, he recalled vividly his first mission.

He had been placed by the Russians in an American foster home. His own parents had been killed when he was five years old. They hadn't wanted to complete a mission to carry out the murder of a predominant oligarch that turned against the previous government. So, they were eliminated. The government realized this was a perfect opportunity to create a sleeper agent. They took the young, parentless boy into their circle. They lavished him with toys and food the likes he never had seen at home. They even provided a mother for him to love and have love returned to compensate for the loss of his own. It didn't take long for the memories of his true parents to fade and a complete connection to his newly found family to take hold.

He then started his lethal training, rewarded each time he would kill some helpless animal. They always started agents with small kills. Insects were the easiest. The pesky bugs could be squashed, stomped on or even drowned. The government closely monitored his reaction to each death. He was rewarded each time he didn't show emotion. Each time, the target grew as did his collection of killing instruments. The man recalled the first cat he had to kill. He never liked to think of the details of that particular instance. But he knew when he did it, not to show any outward feelings. Pushing his emotions down, he carried out the deed with cold, heartless precision. To this day, those emotions only emerged when he was alone, and they materialized through quiet sobbing in dark rooms.

His first human test was his foster parent. It was a man who had been a CIA employee. His work within the agency had him tracking the cybercrimes of the Russian government. He had been tracking a particular government crime ring involving the spying on of American banks. He was getting close to uncovering the ring, so it was decided that he needed to be stopped. The boy's handler instructed him precisely how to carry out the deed. He was to place eye drops in the man's coffee each morning. The eye drops contained tetrahydrozoline, an ingredient known to cause rapid heart rate and confusion if ingested in large quantities over a long period of time. It took about two months for the effects of the drug to start working on his foster dad. After his foster dad's death, he was placed in another foster home. However, this home was run by the Russian government. He was, in his mind, back home. His reward for getting rid of the American threat was a Walther P99 with silencer. This wasn't a practice gun or one that had only been borrowed for his target practice. This was his very own gun. It quickly became his favorite reward and he practiced with it constantly until he could hit his target in almost total darkness from twenty yards out. He reached across the passenger seat and lovingly caressed the cold steel of his old friend.

As the man turned into the cul-de-sac of his undercover neighborhood, he turned off his headlights. He didn't want to alert Crane to his presence. He pulled the car to the cover of the Thula and switched off the ignition. He reached for the gun. "Come on, old friend," he whispered. "We have a job to do" and got out of the car. Quietly, he closed the driver's door. He made a quick look around the still neighborhood. He didn't expect any interruptions, but he wasn't sure relatives wouldn't soon be coming in to take care of their deceased loved one and their belongings.

Deftly, he walked up Crane's driveway to the sidewalk leading to the front steps. He walked to the side of the steps so as not to make any squeaking sounds from any loose boards. He could see movement beyond the oval glass window embedded in the steel door. Crane looked as if he were in the kitchen. *Good*, the man thought. It would take him a couple of seconds to open the door. The perfect amount of time for him to prepare himself with the silencer. He reached out and knocked on the door.

Startled, Dawson jumped at the sound of the knock. He wondered who it could be at this hour. Not that it was very late, but late enough not to be a solicitor. Walking towards the door, his eye caught the umbrella stand

and his dad's cane standing amongst the umbrellas. His dad had died of Alzheimer's and his cane was the only thing of his that Dawson kept. It reminded him of what happened to a once strong man and how he was stricken down by such a debilitating disease. He guessed the two deaths he saw today and seeing the cane made him miss his dad that much more.

Glancing at the umbrella stand, he absentmindedly swung the door open. Much to his relief, it was just one of his neighbors, Alex. "Alex!" He exclaimed excitedly. Happy to see a familiar face. Dawson was ready to spill out all the information he had just witnessed when he saw the gun.

Alex's predetermined aim had been directed at Dawson's heart, and he pulled the trigger as soon as the door swung open to Dawson's surprised face. *Click*. Nothing. Shocked, Alex realized his trusted pistol had failed him. *It couldn't be jammed*, he thought. It was an old gun sure, but he had always taken great care of it. He aimed again at Dawson but not before Dawson's internal flight or fight instincts took over. Seeing Alex distracted by the dismay of his gun not firing, Dawson reached for his dad's cane. At once, he swung the cane with such force, Alex dropped to his knees. Dawson swung again, striking Alex in his temple. Blood started to ooze from the gash on the side of his head as Alex fell to the porch's landing.

Too stunned to ask questions, Dawson immediately grabbed his phone and car keys. He bolted out of the house but not before kicking away the gun that had flown from Alex's hands when he hit the floor. Realizing he had left his laptop, he ran back inside the house, stepping over Alex's unconscious body and grabbed it. He didn't know why he thought of taking the computer, but something deep in his subconscious mind told him to.

He raced to his car, sped out of the driveway, and down the street. He didn't know where he was heading, but he knew he had to get far away. The drone's signal transmitted all that had unfolded beneath it. Tomlin slammed his fist on the table witnessing the scene the tiny camera had revealed on the screen in front of him.

"Go get him." He grunted to his colleague. "Go get him before somebody finds him lying there." He stormed out of the room.

CHAPTER ELEVEN

Andriy slumped in his chair after sending the email. It was as if a heavy burden had been lifted off his shoulders. He slowly began to relax as he watched Fedir sleep. He thought about what to do next. He had been solely concentrating on getting to the lab and sending Crane the information, he hadn't thought about his next moves. He guessed he should get Fedir to the Polish border so he could be looked after. Andriy was still a soldier, and he couldn't perform his duties with a child tagging along. He was also a scientist. He could stay here at the lab and concentrate on finding a counter action to the chemicals he had discovered. He would need to find another power source. The portable propane generators would not last very long if he had to use the lab equipment.

He wondered if he should try to get to the Capital, but that was too far away. President Bagan would want to know, in person, what he had found. He also wasn't sure the President was still in the Capital. Emails could be intercepted, and he didn't want to take that chance. He needed to give him the same information he relayed to Crane hoping they could get in touch with the Americans to help find a treatment or possibly an antidote. Andriy wondered how he could possibly discover an antidote, much less how he would be able to distribute it. He had no idea how it was even dispersed let alone how it could be combatted. When the Nazi's had used Zyclon B, it was released in the chambers. Death was nearly instantaneous. The Ukrainian civilians surely weren't walking into any chambers. They were out in the open, in the air. *Air!* Andriy sat up straight. *The chemical was airborne! But how,* he wondered. *How could the Zyclon B be airborne yet still lethal enough to kill someone?*

His mind was very tired. His body was very tired as well. He needed to rest. He quietly got up from his chair and started out the door. The maintenance closet would have some blankets and maybe he'd find a pillow too. After retrieving a couple rough, woolen blankets, and as luck would have it, two pillows, he returned to the office. Gently, he lifted Fedir's head and placed one of the pillows under his head and then covered him with a blanket. Fedir slightly stirred at the comfortable disturbance of his sleep and then warmly settled further into the couch.

Andriy didn't want to sleep on the floor, but he didn't want to leave Fedir alone either. He walked to the office next door and, as quickly and quietly as he could, dragged a worn, brown leather couch out into the hallway in front of his office door. He propped the door open so he could see Fedir and placed the couch in Fedir's line of sight should he awaken in the middle of the night and not find Andriy. The couch was light but not light enough that Andriy could carry it easily. He slowly dragged one end of the couch while carrying the other end across the tiled floor. The sound seemed deafening in the eerily quiet building. However, whatever noise Andriy was making didn't stir Fedir from his slumber.

After sitting on the couch and grabbing the other pillow and blanket, Andriy rested on the couch. He stared at Fedir, again wondering how he was going to get him to the border. The border was over 80 kilometers away from the lab. Not far by car, but substantially further on foot. It would be an even longer journey than the one he just completed. He didn't relish the thought of traveling such a distance again, however, the closer he got to Poland, the safer the trip would be. The Russian military wouldn't dare attack Poland, for now.

Surely, he would have a better chance of getting the boy to safety if he had more soldiers with him. He hoped that Ukrainian soldiers would be held up near the major cities, but that didn't seem like the case now. More were probably stationed closer to the Capital to stave off any Russian invasion of their precious city. Maybe he could even get him on an evacuation train, but he couldn't think of any near the lab. There was a train station in Shats'k, but if they were going to travel that far, they might as well just head to the border. Getting to the border would be best for Fedir so Andriy could get going on getting his information to the president without any distractions.

He awoke to a soft pat on his shoulder and Fedir whispering his name. Andriy sat up and rubbed his hands over his face and eyes trying to shake off the fog of deep sleep. He hadn't slept that well in a long time. It was refreshing.

"I'm hungry," Fedir said quietly.

His eyes looked so old to Andriy. He could see that Fedir had slept well too, but reality still stirred behind his gaze. Andriy hoped one day that Fedir would be able to shelve the fear and horror he witnessed. He sighed knowing that the process would take many years to accomplish.

"Let's see if there is anything left in the vending machines or even the office cafeteria." Andriy smiled at the boy and tousled the hair on his head. Those words sparked Fedir's solemn face into a small smile.

Andriy and Fedir left their makeshift beds and walked down the hall. Habit forced them to proceed cautiously even though no harm had come to them in the night. It was still war and there was always a chance a rogue soldier, or even an entire battalion could come upon the lab and find them hiding. Their footsteps sounded like echoing drumbeats in the quiet hallway. Without realizing it, both softened their steps.

As they rounded one corner, they saw a vending machine. Andriy knew this to be one of many throughout the building, but it was the closest. The machine they discovered was off a corridor that connected the office clerks' cubicle farm. Glancing at the slim variety of items, he quickly assumed the clerks were sugar junkies. Andriy couldn't be sure how long the contents of the vending machine had been sitting, silently waiting to be chosen. He guessed maybe three months, trying to recall when the employees had totally evacuated the building as the Russian army announced its invasion. He didn't need him or the boy to get food poisoning from any contaminated food even if it would have been a delicious snack at first. The contents of the machine were scarce. There were three chocolate bars with peanuts, two packages of frosted donuts, and six snack bags of potato chips. Again, not very nutritious, but sustainable for their hunger for now. He had used what little change he had to purchase their snacks last night and now needed to figure out how to get these items out of the machine.

Not wanting to damage the precious commodities inside prevented him from taking a chair and throwing it into the glass front. He looked the machine over to find how the parts were connected. Finding screws along the side of the machine that connected a molded steel frame around the glass, he searched for something to loosen the screws. Discovering a drawer with miscellaneous cutlery, he took out a butter knife to use as a screwdriver. Loosening all ten screws, he used the knife again to pry the frame away from the glass. Finally, he was able to lift the glass and expose the snacks. Grabbing all that he could, he gave some to Fedir to carry as well and they hurried back to their makeshift sleeping quarters. He didn't want to feel exposed in the hallways any longer than he had to.

Once back at their rest stop, Andriy looked over the packages. He threw out the donuts, assured that they had to have mold on them by now. He gave Fedir most of the rest to eat, saving just a package or two for himself. He knew he needed to find him and the boy more to eat, and something to drink. He wasn't sure how long he planned on staying in the lab for shelter, but for the moment, it felt good not to think about flying bullets or decaying bodies in the street.

"Why don't we discover what has been left behind to see if it will be useful to us?" he asked Fedir between bites of the candy bar.

"What kind of stuff?" Fedir inquired.

"I don't know for sure, really. I guess we can look in offices and see if we can find something better for me to sleep on and maybe some more food and something to drink." Andriy mused.

He honestly had no idea what he was searching for, but he couldn't just sit there all day either.

They each finished one snack and headed down the quiet passageways again, this time their steps not as cautious as they had been previously. Passing a half-empty trash can, Andriy lifted the plastic bag out and dumped the contents back into the metal can. He needed something to carry their findings in. He repeated this process two more times as they continued their search. He thought about going into the lab and trying to figure out if an antibody could be mapped from the information he had found out about the chemical compound. He mainly was searching for anything that would keep his mind off the war outside. He had heard some bombs in the middle of the night. Given how distant they sounded, he figured the enemy was about twenty to thirty miles away. That wasn't far enough for his liking, but he wasn't quite ready to start the journey to the Polish border.

He decided to go up to the next floor where the corporate offices were. If he remembered correctly, the President, Vice-President, and Chief Financial Officer of the company kept offices up there. Trying to make a game, he raced Fedir up the two flights of stairs. He let the boy win. Mainly because the boy was very weak from not eating properly. Andriy had to find something more substantial for the kid.

Once out of the stairwell, he looked left and right trying to recall where the lavish offices were. He decided to move down the left of the stairwell. Passing a door marked "Private", he paused. He tried the handle on the door and found it unlocked. Cautiously, he turned the handle. Both his and the boy's eyes grew wide as they peered inside the room.

The room was indeed one to be kept private. Andriy flipped the light switch and the generator in the basement started up again. A soft glow of lights revealed a room the size of a small apartment. Beige Berber carpet covered the floors, silencing their steps immediately. To the left, two, soft brown leather sofas formed an L shaped area complete with a mahogany coffee table. Picture books adorned the top of the table making for a quaint sitting area to read. Behind the sofas was a kitchenette area equipped with a large stainless-steel refrigerator, microwave oven and a dishwasher. Eight white cabinets hung on the wall and an additional eight cabinets were underneath the black granite countertop. To the right of the entrance, was another sitting area containing two more leather sofas. This area also had three pieces of gym equipment; a rowing machine, a treadmill and a small weight bench complete with bars and free weights.

Andriy noticed a hallway and carefully proceeded down through it, surprisingly discovering a bathroom complete with a walk-in shower. Checking the vanity of the sink, he noticed shampoo, soap, and towels. He could hardly contain his excitement. He didn't know whether to jump in the shower or check out the kitchen first. He decided they both needed food first.

Heading back to the kitchen, he and Fedir explored each cabinet. The occupants of the private office must have been to the store not long before they evacuated the building. Each cabinet was filled with food. They had their choice of canned vegetables, dried pastas and rice, cereal, shelf-stable milk and packaged meats. Holding down the urge to eat everything at once, they opened the refrigerator to find several bottles of water and beer. Andriy felt as if he had hit the jackpot!

"Let's eat!" Andriy said, smiling as he faced the boy. Fedir let out a squeal of delight. "Be careful though, we don't want to eat too much at once and get ourselves sick," Andriy cautioned.

Fedir nodded his head in agreement at the same time he tried to quiet his growling stomach.

Andriy some of the containers of milk in the refrigerator to get them cold. He didn't want to drink warm milk if he didn't have to. He had a feeling that they would be staying in this room for the remainder of their time here. Hungrily, he prepared some rice for them to eat in the microwave.

Ten minutes later, he and Fedir were sitting on the couch eating their bowls of rice and some Vienna sausages he had found. Luckily. none of the food was expired. He figured they would have enough for about two weeks and that's how long he planned on staying. They both needed to calm their nerves, rest, and prepare for the journey ahead. He wondered how anyone could survive in a constant state of fear for days, even months, on end.

Finishing up their meals, Andriy cleaned off the bowls and placed them in the dishwasher. Walking down the hall to the bathroom, he noticed another closed door off the hallway he hadn't seen. He must have missed it in the excitement of discovering the shower. He opened the door to find a bedroom. It had two full-sized beds complete with sheets, a comforter, and pillows. "Fedir!" he happily exclaimed.

Fedir raced down the hall stopping just short of Andriy. When he saw what Andriy was looking at, he bolted past him and flopped on one of the beds. Turning over, he faced Andriy and simply grinned.

"Good idea," Andriy said, reading his mind. He promptly fell on the other bed and within minutes, they both were fast asleep.

CHAPTER TWELVE

Stephanie lay on the hospital cot, staring at the pointed dome of the tent. The slightest movement caused waves of nausea, so she dared not move. Even her eyes were locked, fixed on the center pole. She wasn't alone. Several nurses were in the tent with her in various stages of the mysterious illness. She had been in her cot for the past three days, only risking movement to pick ice chips from her cup and bring them to her mouth. She needed to stay hydrated. Some of the nurses were starting to get better and could sit up now. They were able to eat small meals without throwing up. Stephanie prayed for the time to pass so she could do the same.

While incapacitated, she thought back to the moments that led up to her sickness. She recalled soldiers being brought into the tent; their skin blotched with dark blisters. She heard talk among the sick nurses that most of them had died. Some recovered however, and she wondered why. What did all this mean? She was an over-analyzing person when it came to things she didn't understand. Contrary to what Dawson had thought about her *go with the flow* personality, when something didn't add up, she would spend hours trying to pinpoint what exactly was happening. To her, it was like putting together a jigsaw puzzle. She would take each piece and try to fit it into the overall puzzle until a picture would emerge.

The conversations she overheard, even with her broken Polish understanding, led her to realize that the severity of the soldiers' illnesses was in direct correlation to the region they had come from. The further away they were from a small town near Kiev called Brovary, the less severe their condition. Neither Stephanie nor the nurses developed any blisters which was also another interesting puzzle piece. She also didn't recall any soldier who had come in directly from the town in question.

After another two days, Stephanie was feeling much better. She wasn't back to her full self by any means, but she was well enough to start slowly eating solid foods. The other nurses who were where she was, physically, a few days ago, were back in the main tents of the hospital. Back to treating the sick and injured soldiers. Stephanie was only one of a handful of aids and nurses left in the tent that had not fully recovered. Since there weren't any new nurses on staff or volunteering, she gathered that when the remaining patients in the tent were recovered enough, they could convert the tent back into a full triage tent again. It was as if the nausea tsunami that had taken over the nurses was now a calm wave, not making any new splashes. She also noticed from the conversations she had with others, that the nurses who had experienced the illness were not getting sick again after treating more soldiers with the blisters. Another piece of the puzzle was coming together in Stephanie's mind.

Talking to the nurses on her road to recovery, she learned more about the town of Brovary. It was located about 26 kilometers outside of Kiev. Stephanie did the conversion in her head; about 16 miles. Close enough to Kiev but not a highly sought-after town, like Mariupol had been in the previous war. Before the previous war, Brovary was famous for its beer. Travelers would often stop in the town to taste the local brews manufactured there.

After the war, the town thrived again. The breweries' production skyrocketed. Brovary became well known globally as it began to export their famous beers to thirsty customers across the world. People wanted to forget the invasion and celebrate the overthrowing of the Russian government by one of its own generals. Little did they suspect their celebrations would turn to mourning.

Stephanie wondered if the wheat and barley of the region was causing the soldiers to become ill. She had never heard of such a thing. She thought about Dawson again. He would be able to figure this out. He was a better analyzer than she was, she had to admit. She found herself thinking a lot about Dawson lately. She started questioning why she left in the first place. Was their relationship that bad? Was she so focused on being a free spirit that she couldn't fathom a life with roots? Or what is it her that was afraid of the commitment? The commitment to one person for the rest of her life. Yes, that's what scared her the most. Instead of talking to Dawson about it, she bolted. Just like her dad did.

Stephanie's mom had always been the responsible one. She took care of the house, the finances, the grocery shopping, and everything else that needed to be done in a marriage, in a healthy relationship. Her dad worked to do his supportive part with the finances, but he never paid a bill in his life. When he'd come home from work, he just wanted to play. Play with Stephanie, play on his phone, play on his computer. Anything other than his responsibilities of being the proverbial man of the house. He hated anything that had to do with the upkeep of the house, of the lawn or even sitting at the maintenance shops to get oil changes on the cars.

Stephanie remembered going on walks with her dad through various state parks. They would pack up the car on a Saturday morning and drive two or three hours looking for the perfect park. She was too young to recall the names and they weren't important. What was important was holding her dad's hand as they walked unpaved trails. They'd stop when they saw any type of movement, crouching down on their knees to watch baby deer walk through the woods swishing their tails making their way through the dense thicket. Or the time he brought along makeshift fishing poles. They were simply long sticks with a string tied on and a bent wire at the other end. He'd dig in the forest dirt until he'd find a worm, hook it, and then toss it into the stream. More times than not, nothing was ever caught. Occasionally, however, one misguided fish would be enticed enough to get itself hooked on the line. Stephanie would clap her hands in delight and laugh at the poor fish frantically flailing for its freedom until it wiggled itself off of the makeshift hook. Those memories made her smile now. But she also remembered the fighting.

Her mom would constantly nag her dad to do chores, paint, or fix something broken. Her mom's voice rose in volume as he would say "I'll get to it later" and never did. Her mom had to almost break down in tears before her father would realize that she had had enough and only then would he begrudgingly do whatever she needed done. Until one day, he didn't. He just left. Stephanie realized she was doing the same thing to Dawson her dad did to her mom; always wanting the fun stuff and never wanting the responsibility.

Dawson's work was very important to him, she realized. She would tell him this if he even spoke to her. She wasn't very nice when she left, and she didn't say very nice things to him while in the process of leaving. She needed to explain to him how wrong she was. She hoped she'd get the chance soon. With the war, she couldn't see that happening. She prayed he wouldn't move on with someone else.

She sighed to herself. She wasn't going to wallow in self-pity. The nurses and doctors needed her. The soldiers needed her. She was determined not to let them down.

CHAPTER THIRTEEN

Dawson didn't know where he was headed to. He just knew he had to get far away from the house and from Alex. *Alex!* Why did Alex want to kill him? Alex had always been the fun one of the group. *When did he become a cold-blooded killer?* Dawson's thoughts were frantic as he tried to figure out what role Alex played in all this. *Did he have something to do with Bob and Tom's death? How could he have even known about that?* He was out of town, or so Dawson thought. His mind screamed for answers he just could not provide. He needed to find a place to think. He decided to drive another hour just to feel safe. Safe enough to gather his thoughts. He didn't even know who to contact about all this. The events that took place left him suspicious of everyone and everything.

He pulled his car into a small motel parking lot with a vacancy sign on the marquee. The man at the front desk looked up from his newspaper, perturbed by the interruption.

"Can I help you?" he snidely asked Dawson.

"I'd like a room for the night, please," Dawson calmly stated.

"That'll be fifty bucks. Cash only!" grunted the man. Dawson handed him the money and took the key offered. The man didn't even tell him the room number; he had to look at the key to determine that. Dawson walked out of the tiny, dust covered office, hoping his room would be in better condition, as the man returned to his newspaper.

Finding his room not too far from where he parked his car, Dawson entered the room and reached to turn on the lights. He was surprised to find the room clean and comfortable looking. He quickly closed the door behind him, once again reminded of the reason he was there in the first place. He sat down on the bed just for a second before springing to his feet. He realized he had left his computer in the car. Quickly, he exited the room and walked to his car. He opened the car door and reached inside to retrieve his computer. Suddenly, he noticed a faint red flashing light under his driver seat. He had never seen that before, but he also never went to his car in the pitch darkness he was in now of this remote motel parking lot. A chill raced down Dawson's spine and his flight instinct kicked into gear.

He swiftly pulled at the red light, his fingers grasping thin wires. He yanked until he pulled the light out from underneath his seat. The light went out immediately. The car's overhead light showed Dawson a tiny lens and the chill returned to his spine. This wasn't right. He threw the light and wires as far away from his car as he could. Feeling around the underside of his car, he felt a small box. Carefully, he pulled the box from its hiding place. It must have dislodged when he pulled the other wires. There was a light still blinking on this. Holding it in his hand, he looked around at the scarce number of cars in the parking lot. He found a green sedan similar to his own with out-of-state plates. He carefully placed the box under the wheel housing surrounding the rear driver side wheel. He relaxed some when he heard the click of the magnet meeting steel securing the box in place. The drone's transmission immediately broadcasted static, and the tracking recording stopped.

The auxiliary tracker was still functional and still sending the tracking, but it showed a slightly different location than the primary one before it went offline. Sergei tapped on the screens to try to bring the main tracker back online, but it wasn't working. He reached for his cellphone to call the incident in and then paused. He had been watching the unfolding of events of the man he was assigned to watch after that initial email had come through. He didn't like what was happening. He thought the initial assignment was to simply track the American and report his whereabouts. The email, the house surveillance, and now the death of the American's neighbors started to give Sergei a funny feeling, and he didn't like the path his conclusions were leading him to. He decided, for now, not to notify his superiors about the glitch, hoping the main feed would resume when Dawson next started the car.

Stepping away from the car, Dawson re-entered his motel room. He sat there on the bed deciding what to do next. Obviously, someone was watching him, or at least his movements, but who? His gut told him that he was on the right track by replacing the tracker even though he wasn't one hundred percent sure why. Maybe he thought he could throw whoever was looking for him off his trail. He continued those thoughts. Gathering his stuff, he left the room, got into his car, and drove away from the motel.

Dawson wasn't truly concentrating on where he was going. Some part of his brain focused on the road and any cars; the other part focused on what to do next. He surmised he couldn't go home; that was a given. He also didn't think it would be wise to go into the office but that's where he was heading. Before he arrived at his destination, he made a few stops along the way.

His first stop was to an ATM to withdraw some cash. He subconsciously thought that doing so would trigger his location, but he needed cash. The ATM was within walking distance of the motel, so maybe his trackers would think he walked there since the car with the box was still parked at the motel. He then went just a little further to a convenience store and bought some snacks and toiletries, using his credit card. He hoped all these transactions would show he was where they could safely find him. He knew he wasn't well versed in clandestine operations, but he had seen enough spy movies to try to see If this would work.

Getting back into his car, he continued his journey to the office. He wasn't sure who he could trust, but maybe one of the investors could help him out. He decided to call Agent Tomlin. His number was on Dawson's business card holder in his office. Tomlin seemed the most logical person to report this to since he was working with Dawson's lab and the lab in Ukraine. He had even transferred some of his own people over there when ChemComm started their investigation into the chemical warfare allegations from Andriy's email, which Dawson at the time, thought was a great idea.

By the time his people got to Lutsk Labs, Andriy had left. Tomlin's people did report; however, notes were left from the research he had done during his brief stay in the lab. Tomlin had told Dawson Andriy had left to get to the Polish border. Tomlin had even told him that Andriy had picked up a small boy who had been orphaned when his parents were killed at the start of the war. Tomlin could be trusted, Dawson surmised.

Dawson hoped that Andriy and the boy made it to Poland safely. His racing thoughts paused for a moment at the notion of Poland. His mind turned to Stephanie as the place and the person became synonymous to him. He hoped she was doing okay. He wondered if she joined in the cause at the Polish border. She most likely would since she was that type of person. Regret creeped into his thoughts, and he considered, briefly, taking a flight to Poland to see her. Maybe he had been mistaken in letting the relationship end.

Snapping back to reality, Dawson realized he was close to the office. His musings had diminished his driving concentration and he found himself pulling into the company's parking garage. Parking close to the elevator, he examined his surroundings before getting out of his car. The garage was practically empty with the few cars there probably belonging to the evening cleaning crew.

He reached the elevators and started to use his badge to gain entry. He stopped short of tapping the keypad. *What if my badge is being tracked?* He thought. His mind started racing with all the possibilities of how he could be noticed. He backed away from the elevator and looked around the garage again. His heart was pounding in his chest and his mind started reeling. *I'm being followed. I'm being tracked. Who can I trust? Can I truly trust Tomlin? Who killed my neighbors?* All these questions bombarded his thoughts. He decided to get back into his car and drive as far away as he could from the lab. Something in his gut told him the lab was the first place whoever was tracking him would look. He'd have to find another way to get in contact with Tomlin.

Leaving the garage, Dawson decided to find another obscure hotel to rest. He drove about a half hour before he found the perfect spot. It was a bit off the main road. The sign for the motel's name had half the letters in its neon letters shorted out. He walked into the lobby that was more like an old office converted into a registration booth. The walls were paneled in a faux wood design left over from the 1970's. The air smelled musty from a leaky window covered in a slight grime that probably didn't let enough light in during the day. The attendee behind the glass enclosure was a heavy-set man in a blue shirt and a mustache that should have been trimmed a week ago along with the wiry stubble of his beard. He lunged forward in his seat when Dawson walked in, and the bell alerted the clerk to his presence. He had been eating a sub sandwich and watching TV when the noise disturbed him.

Standing up to greet his customer, he said, "Can I help you?" Having not taken the time to swallow his food, Dawson didn't immediately understand what he had just said.

Assuming he inquired about Dawson needing a room, Dawson replied, "I'd like a room for two nights." The clerk wiped his hands on his shirt and reached for a clipboard with the registration papers for Dawson to fill out.

"We only take cash," snarled the man, as he handed Dawson the paperwork. "And we don't allow any guests in the room without them being checked in too," he added with a tone in his voice that suggested the motel tended to be used by questionable clientele.

"No problem," Dawson answered. "It's just me." He turned away from the clerk and sat down to fill out the paperwork. Looking over the information boxes to be completed, Dawson decided to use a fake name and address. Since he was paying cash, he guessed the clerk wouldn't ask him for any identification. He finished filling out the paperwork and handed it back to the clerk.

Barely glancing at any of the information, he looked up at Dawson and simply said, "That'll be a hundred dollars for both nights, paid in advance." Dawson handed him a hundred-dollar bill which he promptly held up to the dingy lights in the room. Dawson wanted to tell him that's not how you checked for a fake bill, but he refrained from doing so. The man put the money in his cash drawer and handed Dawson a worn-out plastic keychain and a brass key. "Room 103," the man barked turning back to his movie.

Dawson found his room, inserted the key, and entered. It smelled as musty as the office did, but by this time of the night, he was just too exhausted to care. Locking the door behind him, he pushed the curtains back to survey the parking lot. Not finding anything suspicious, he turned back toward the room and walked over to the bed. He plopped down on the bed, not even removing his clothes and fell fast asleep. When he woke, he picked up his phone. He had decided on a plan.

CHAPTER FOURTEEN

Andriy's slumber was interrupted by a sound he couldn't quite make out. It sounded like scratching. After his first unexpected encounter with Fedir, he slept very lightly. At first, he thought that mice or rats had gotten into the building scavenging for food, but the sounds were further off. Quietly, he got up from his makeshift bed, picked up his gun, and made his way into the hallway to follow the sound. The echoes from the corridors made it difficult to pinpoint the direction of the sound. Turning this way and that, he finally found himself in the main entryway to the building. The sound was coming from outside the front door.

Trying to discern the scratching, his heart started racing. He envisioned many things trying to get into the building. *Could it be a wounded soldier desperately clawing to get in? If it were a soldier, what side was he on?* It could also be a wild animal. Wolves were known to the area and Andriy speculated that any number of them could be scavenging for food since their natural habitats were most likely destroyed.

By the time he reached the door, the scratching had stopped. *Maybe it was a wild animal*, he thought, *and it decided to move on.*

Still, Andriy wanted to check the outside. As he reached for the door, the scratching returned. The sound of the scratching starting again made him jump in fear. He faintly heard whining along with the claws, or whatever it was, on the door. Gauging where the sound was, it was low to the ground. Ever so slightly, he opened the door. Gazing down, he saw a small dog. He let out a sigh of relief.

Andriy opened the door, and the dog came bounding in, wagging its tail. Andriy bent down to hold the dog still. He didn't want it running away from him into the building. The dog immediately nuzzled itself against Andriy. He was a medium-sized dog, probably around twenty-five pounds had it been fully nourished. Its fur appeared to be a coarse-brown texture, but it was hard to tell given how dirty it was.

As Andriy petted the dog, he could feel its ribs. The dog seemed to enjoy the petting, and licked Andriy's face to show its appreciation. He guessed the breed to be some sort of wired-hair terrier. He never had a dog growing up, but his family members did, and he always enjoyed watching dog shows airing from America.

"Okay, okay!" he said to the dog, smiling as it continued to lick his face. "Let's see if we can find you something to eat."

Andriy stood up and attempted to pick the dog up, but it walked ahead of him sensing where they needed to go. Walking a few steps behind the dog, he noticed it was a male. He also noticed the dog appeared to be looking around the surroundings as if searching for something. As they continued down the hallway, the dog would stop and turn to Andriy as if to make sure he was still there. He'd then continue his walk. When they got to the end of the hallway and needed to make a turn to continue, the dog stopped and looked back at Andriy again as if to ask for directions. Andriy simply nodded his head to the right. The dog turned to the right and continued his path.

Andriy thought that maybe the dog was someone's pet. He wasn't afraid of humans, he was very friendly, and he seemed trained. *How else would a dog understand a head nod for direction?*

He put the thought aside for the moment as he thought about, instead, how Fedir would react to the dog. He smiled as he imagined the boy's delight at seeing the dog. *The boy sure could use something happy in life*, he mused.

Closing in on the office where Fedir was sleeping, Andriy whispered "stop" to the dog. Immediately, the dog stopped. Andriy stepped in front of the dog and entered the office. The dog did not move. Fedir was still sleeping peacefully. Andriy didn't want to wake him, but he also wanted to see the boy's reaction to their newfound friend. He turned to the dog with a finger on his lips and waved the dog inside. The dog understood this command as well, and quietly entered the room. He walked over to Fedir's sleeping form and sniffed him. His cold nose must have touched Fedir because he began to stir. The dog's excitement was apparent from his wagging tail. It was as if he was anticipating this moment as much as Andriy was.

Fedir groggily opened his eyes. When his vision focused on the dog, his eyes immediately widened. The excitement was contagious, and the dog jumped on the bed with Fedir licking his face as Fedir squealed with delight. Andriy smiled at the scene before him. He felt as if he had given Fedir the best Christmas present of his young life. The scene choked Andriy up and he had to clear his throat to keep himself from crying.

"Where did you find him?" Fedir asked through laughter.

"He was scratching at the main door," Andriy answered. "He's very hungry and very dirty," he added. "I think we need to get him something to eat and then give him a bath, or rather, a shower."

"Can we keep him?" Fedir sheepishly asked.

Andriy couldn't find a reason to say no. The boy was obviously delighted at the presence of the dog, and he didn't want to crush his happiness.

"I don't see why not. He may be someone's pet, but we have no way of knowing where to find his owners," he said. "I'm going to see if I can find him something he can eat. While I'm doing that, why don't you think of a name for him? After he eats, you and I will get him cleaned up." Andriy turned towards the office kitchen to search for something for the dog.

Andriy found some canned tuna fish in the cabinet. After checking the expiration dates again to be sure, he opened the can and poured it into a bowl. The smell of the fish must have caught the dog's attention because he came bounding into the kitchen and sat down next to Andriy. Andriy put the bowl down, but the dog just sat there looking up at him.

Confused that the dog wasn't eating, Andriy said, "Eat!"

The dog immediately bent down to the bowl and started eating. *He must be someone's pet*, Andriy thought again.

He got some water from the sink and put that in a bowl as well and sat it next to the dog. After he finished eating, the dog drank all the water in the bowl. Andriy put some more water in the bowl, and he drank almost half of it before he stopped and looked back up at Andriy.

"Come on, boy," he said and started over to Fedir. "Well, he was definitely hungry and very thirsty," Andriy said as they entered the living area. "Have you come up with a name for him?" he asked.

Fedir shook his head. "I've never had a dog before. What happens if I give him the wrong name?", he asked sincerely.

"You can't give a dog a wrong name," Andriy chuckled. "Just name him the first thing that comes to your mind."

"Okay." Fedir sat there for a minute longer, brow furrowed as if in deep thought. "I think I'm going to name him Zeus," he said resoundingly. "I like that name. It's a Greek god we were learning about in school." His voice softened at the memory of his school and the events that happened that fateful day when he was returning home from it.

"That's a great name!" Andriy excitedly said, trying to turn Fedir's thoughts away from the tragedy he was remembering. "How about you and I try to get Zeus into the shower. He stinks!"

Fedir giggled in agreement. He got up and waved for Zeus to follow them. He and Andriy got some towels from the bathroom closet, and closed the door so Zeus couldn't escape.

After cleaning Zeus and drying him off, Fedir played with the dog a little while longer until Zeus got tired and laid down to nap. He and Andriy fixed themselves something to eat and sat down watching the dog sleep as they ate their lunch.

"As much as I would like to stay, and although I think we may be safe, I think we need to start moving out of here," Andriy said as he gathered up Fedir's plate after he finished eating. "I don't want to stay here too much longer and run the risk of the Russians coming here. I feel as if our luck may run out and we won't be prepared."

"Where are we going to go?" Fedir asked sadly.

He liked where they were. It was quiet and comfortable. They had food at the ready. He had a warm place to sleep. He didn't want to leave, but he knew Andriy was right; they couldn't stay much longer.

"We need to get to the Polish border. We'll be safe there," Andriy said with the understanding of Fedir's sadness. He wanted to stay here too, but he knew they couldn't. "I need to get some information I found to the right people. It may save our soldiers," he added.

At the mention of saving soldiers, Fedir straightened up. He loved his country, and he didn't want to see it under the Russians again. He had heard the stories of the war before. He knew that the people of Ukraine would win again, like they did before, but he also knew that a lot of people were being killed and he wanted it to stop.

"Okay!" he said with conviction in his voice. "When do we leave?"

"We'll leave tomorrow. We need to pack some food for us and for Zeus," he said as he patted the dog's head. Zeus seemed to realize what was going on and licked Andriy's hand in agreement. "But, for now, let's just have some time with our new friend. We'll pack up after dinner tonight and leave first thing in the morning."

CHAPTER FIFTEEN

The ringing of the phone woke Stephanie out of her deep sleep. She had been working non-stop it seemed for days and was exhausted.

"Hello," she said, yawning into the phone.

"Stephanie? It's me. Dawson." A familiar voice answered her.

Instantaneously, Stephanie was wide awake. "Dawson!" Fear and excitement mixed in her voice. "Is everything alright?"

She couldn't imagine why Dawson was calling other than to deliver bad news. Sure, she had thought about him often lately, especially with the soldiers and civilians coming into the triage tents with mysterious blisters. *With his background, he'd be all over the illnesses*, she thought. She honestly didn't expect to hear from him again, though.

"I'm okay...for now," he paused. "I may need your help. I don't know where else to turn. I don't want to go into details over the phone, but I think I'm in big trouble. If I can get to Poland, is there any way you can get me from the airport and put me up for a while?" he babbled out quickly.

A sinking feeling came over Stephanie as she answered his question. "What, what kind of trouble, Dawson?" she inquired hesitantly.

"Steph." He started. "Tom and Bob are dead. Alex tried to kill me. The Russian government may be involved. That's all I can say right now.

Please. Can you help me if I can get there? I need to know."

"I guess I could get away to pick you up. When are you trying to get here?" she asked.

"I'm not sure yet. I'm not even sure I can get out of the country."

"What's going on, Dawson?" she asked suspiciously.

"I can't tell you now. You'll just have to trust me." he said tersely. "Look, I can't talk long. I'll call you if I'm able to get a ticket and then I'll give you the information about when I'll be there. I've got to go." Dawson hung up the phone.

Stephanie stared at her phone listening to the dial tone on the other end. *What has Dawson gotten himself into? How did Tom and Bob die? Did he say someone killed them and that Alex tried to kill him?*

Stephanie got out of bed and went into the bathroom to get some water on her face. After drying her face, she paced the tiny room she had been given in the makeshift housing unit erected for the medical staff. Her mind was spinning as she thought about their brief conversation. She wondered if she was in danger as well as Dawson. She wondered if she should tell someone here about what she had learned. Sitting down on the bed, she decided not to mention the phone call to anyone just yet. Until she had more answers from Dawson, it was best that only she knew .

Stephanie arrived at the triage tent to find it only half full of wounded civilians. The soldiers that had been there yesterday were gone. She didn't think most of them were ready to travel yet, but maybe the doctors decided that they needed the space for civilians and sent them to the military hospital over in the next town.

"Hey, Luca. Where did all the soldiers go?" she inquired of her coworker.

"Oh, they sent them off to the military hospital for further treatment. Those blisters seem to be causing a concern to the military brass."

Something was definitely going on and Stephanie had a sinking feeling that Dawson knew exactly what it was. Her pacifist mind could not wrap around the idea that people were out there purposely trying to kill other human beings in a most maniacal way. *Were the Russians using some sort of chemical on the soldiers? Were the civilians just collateral damage?* Her mind raced with the sickening idea that all this was being done premeditatedly. She started to feel nauseous again and excused herself from the room.

After gathering herself in the ladies' latrine, Stephanie stepped back into the tent. Regardless of what plans may be unfolding in this war, the patients still needed her. She also had a foreboding feeling that somehow, someone was going to put her and Dawson together. *I could very well be in danger at this very moment*, she thought.

Paranoia creeped into her thoughts. She tried to push them down. She needed to push them down. She needed to act naturally. She needed to be herself so as to not draw attention. Right now, in this tent, at this moment, she was a nobody. She needed to keep it that way.

Throughout the rest of the day, Stephanie did her best to remain calm. She treated the wounded that came into the tent, made small talk with the injured, cheered up the children as best she could with a sweet treat, and assisted her coworkers when needed. All the while, constantly glancing around her searching for any signs that she was found out.

When her shift was finally over, she made her way back to her secluded room. She had a massive headache from trying to keep herself together. She grabbed her purse to look for some pain relief. When she opened her purse, she found a photograph of her and Cara right when they arrived at the border to help the medical staff. They looked so innocent, so unsuspecting of the horrors they were about to see. She only saw Cara now and then since she had been assigned to a different section of the border's massive makeshift village.

The whole border was lined with tents of various needs. Hospitals, soup kitchens, lodging, bathrooms, men's and women's shower areas, all were contained under thousands of feet of white tops and flaps. The whole installation of the tents took the Polish army about two weeks to construct. And they did it with such precision that not one necessity was overlooked or accounted for. Cara had been assigned to the kitchen tents. Stephanie headed over there at once.

When she arrived at the tent, she heard loud, almost cheerful conversations coming from within. A hot meal and a place to rest was good for the body and mind. She searched the crowd for Cara. It was hard to distinguish anyone from the throngs of people sitting around eating or standing in the line from the kitchen filling up their plates. Stephanie was just about to leave when she spotted Cara near the kitchen entrance talking to a soldier. The closeness of their bodies told her that Cara was doing more than just serving food to this particular one.

Grinning, Stephanie made her way over to the couple. "Hey, there," she said lightheartedly. Cara slowly turned towards Stephanie with a blush creeping into her cheeks.

"Hi!" she said, sheepishly. The soldier excused himself and left Stephanie and Cara alone.

"So, who's the new guy?" Stephanie asked.

"Oh, it's not what you think. He just got here and wanted someone to talk to. Honestly. He came up to me and just started talking." Cara stammered.

"It's okay. It's okay," Stephanie said amusingly. "He is rather cute. I don't blame you." She winked.

"So, what brings you in here tonight? I thought you liked to get away from the crowds once your shift was over." Cara asked.

"Um, huh, I don't know how to say this. I really needed someone to talk to. Is there somewhere quiet we can go?" Stephanie solicited.

"Yeah, give me a second to let someone know I'm going to step out for a minute." Cara turned and walked over to the kitchen staff.

When she returned, she wrapped her arm in Stephanie's and they headed out of the tent. Cara found a small space that wasn't occupied. The space had a barrel with a fire going and a bench to sit on.

They sat down and Stephanie turned to Cara. "I think I need your help," Stephanie started. "Dawson called me this morning. He said he was in trouble and that he was going to try to get here, to Poland. I didn't know who to talk to. I'm so scared for him right now." Her words rushed from her lips. She told Cara what Dawson had briefly told her this morning.

Cara was visibly taken aback by Stephanie's trembling voice. She could see her friend was scared. She put her arms around her shaking body to comfort her.

"Oh, my goodness. What can I do? Do you think they'll come after you too?" Cara whispered; afraid someone would overhear their conversation.

"I don't know. That's why I'm so scared. I mean, not many people know I'm in Poland let alone at the border helping the refugees," she said. "But does that mean they won't find out? Whoever, *they* is."

Cara thought for a moment, "If Dawson can get out of the country, tell him he can stay at my place. I'm here, you're here, and we'll probably be here for some time. He could stay there and that way he'd be away from you and any possible connection."

"Yeah, maybe. I just don't know. You're right though. If he stayed at your place, maybe he could get to the proper authorities with whatever information he has. It just seems like he's hinting that the Russians may have something to do with the deaths if that's even possible. Why would they try to kill Dawson? He has nothing to do with this war," Stephanie said.

"We'll figure this out," Cara offered caringly. "For now, though, why don't you and I get something to eat? We got an international shipment today. They're having comfort food tonight; baked chicken, mashed potatoes, and cherry pie. If that can't cheer you up, nothing can!"

They left the bench and headed back into the tent. The idea of food and something warm improved Stephanie's mood and she looked forward to filling her belly.

CHAPTER SIXTEEN

Dawson and Stephanie's brief conversation set off alarms and Sergei was the one to intercept them again. Once they had locked on to Crane, all of his electronic devices were hacked, and tracking software had been silently installed. He listened to Dawson's summary that his neighbors were dead, and that Alex had tried to kill him. Something wasn't sitting right with Sergei. He knew he should alert his supervisor to the incident along with the failed tracking transmission, but something held him back.

Sergei had been a young boy during the last war. However, he wasn't too young to remember the horrors that his countrymen had inflicted on the Ukrainians. After the war, there was peace between the two countries. No one suspected that General Gorsky would try to take back control of Ukraine. When he had succeeded in his coup, he had done so with the promise that he would unite the two countries again, vowing never to invade. The Russian people backed his coup and sang his praises when he toppled the previous leaders. The borders had been reopened and families were reunited. Sergei's sister met a Ukrainian while she attended the university and they married shortly afterwards. Sergei adored his nieces, and he was godfather to them both.

He didn't want to see another war. He didn't want to see the borders closed again. He didn't want to see families torn apart, and he certainly didn't want to see the Ukrainian people subjected to the horrors of whatever General Gorsky was unleashing in the country. He needed to help the American. He decided he would only give his superiors enough information to keep track of the American, but not every detail. Sergei knew if he tried to go to the American authorities with the information he had, he would undoubtedly be killed, along with his entire family as well.

He would let them know that Crane was trying to get to Poland. They would immediately try to stop him by creating some false claim that he was a terrorist threat and be placed on a no-fly list. Sergei couldn't stop that from happening, but maybe he could find another way to help him.

Dawson's phone rang almost immediately after he had hung up with Stephanie. He didn't recognize the phone number and was hesitant to answer it.

"Hello?" It was a question, not an acknowledgment.

"Mr. Crane. You don't know me, but we need to talk" said a male voice on the other end of the line with a thick Russian accent.

"Who is this?" Dawson asked suspiciously.

"My name is Sergei. I've been tracking you for days now. I know about your neighbors. I know about the tracker being removed from your car. I know where you are right now." He didn't sound threatening, just very matter of fact.

Dawson felt his mouth go dry and his knees began to shake. "Don't worry, Mr. Crane. I'm on your side," Sergei added.

"How do I know you're on my side, as you say?" Still unsettled by the unexpected phone call.

"Mr. Crane. I was hired by the Russian government to track your moves. A job I thought was simply to observe and report your movements. Then the incident with your neighbors happened. Then Alex went to your house. There have been documents coming from your emails, and those of Andriy Koval. I have been privy to those documents. I can put two and two together, and I don't like what they add up to. I want to help you, but you must trust me," Sergei said.

Dawson didn't know what to do or say next. Could this man really be trying to help him or could it all be a trap. "Why do you want to help me?" Dawson's question gave a slight hint to his willingness to trust Sergei.

"Because I don't want my family to die," Sergei simply said. "My government has, or appears to have, violated the Geneva Convention. Don't be surprised, Mr. Crane, I know all about the Geneva Convention," Sergei added when he heard Crane's slight intake of breath. "I cannot watch my fellow countrymen suffer while I do absolutely nothing. In fact, I would be helping to destroy them."

Dawson was silent for a moment. His next words would decide his fate. One miscalculation on his part could mean his death. He took a deep breath. "I need to get to Poland. Andriy knows what this chemical is, and the Ukrainian government needs to know too," he said, sealing his fate.

"I can help you with that," Sergei said matter-of-factly. "Right now, my government is sending forces out to neutralize you. They will be watching the airports, in fact, you're probably on a no-fly list as we speak concocted by the Russian government listing you as a possible domestic terrorist. I can get you a new passport and identification papers as soon as tomorrow. Can you keep yourself safe and undetected until then?"

"I believe I can," Dawson said. "I found the other tracker on my car and removed it. It's now stuck to a car at the hotel I was at when I first found it. The car had out of state plates, so maybe they'll follow it." *I hope they don't hurt the people driving the car when they find out they're not me*, Dawson thought. "I also made purchases around the other hotels that were within walking distance, so they'd think that I was still there," he told Sergei.

Sergei was impressed. "Great ideas. Give me the address of where you are staying, and I will overnight the documents you need. You don't have a lot of time to practice your new identity, so do the best you can. I will try to send you an identity card close to your name. I can't make any promises though."

"Great. Hey, I appreciate what you're doing. I'm so scared right now. But, moreover, I'm mad. If what I think is going on is really happening, these people must be stopped. So many people died during World War II to the monsters that ran those camps. Innocent people. Innocent!" Dawson's anger was rising.

"Mr. Crane. Again, I'm on your side," Sergei said. "I lost relatives in that war. In those camps. Relatives that I could have known. Relatives that could have helped shape our country into a better place. My great-grandmother was 18 when she was sent to those camps even though her grandfather was Russian. They didn't care; she had Jewish blood and that was enough to encamp her. She had just married my great-grandfather, and she was pregnant. Luckily, she wasn't in the camp for long before it was liberated, and she lived. My great-grandfather wasn't so lucky. He was killed two days after arriving at Auschwitz." Dawson could hear the hurt in Sergei's weighted words. "I can't see that happen again."

"I'm so sorry," was all Dawson could say. Redirecting the conversation, Dawson added, "I need to let someone at ChemComm know what's going on. There's a guy named Harold Tomlin that has been notified of the email from Andriy. He has sent out a search party to get Andriy out of Ukraine to safety so he can work on some sort of antidote to the chemical. I can let him know that I'm heading to Poland to meet up with Andriy," Dawson remarked.

"Mr. Crane. I need to end this call before my superiors come back. Please be ready to leave when you get the documents from me. And whatever you do, do not contact Harold Tomlin."

With that, Sergei disconnected the call.

CHAPTER SEVENTEEN

The next morning, Andriy and Fedir prepared to leave the lab. They both took showers wondering when they would be able to do so again. The warm water felt good on Andriy's body. His muscles had stiffened up last night. His sleep had been disruptive. His mind kept imagining the horrors they were about to face again. He wondered if he could keep himself and the boy safe for the journey. He wondered if they would be able to pack enough food and supplies to sustain them should they find themselves in need of shelter along the way. He estimated that it would take the pair approximately ten days to reach the border by foot. *Too long,* he mused. *Too long.*

He got out of the shower, dried off and got dressed. He decided against wearing his army uniform. If they could disguise themselves as refugees, maybe they would have a better chance of making it to the border. Then again, he would not be able to disguise his weapons. He had been issued a standard military assault rifle, a Bowie-style knife, and Glock 26 9mm pistol. His uniform was equipped to carry these weapons with its various pockets and holsters, civilian clothes wouldn't give him any options. The office suite has not only been stocked with all the luxuries of a hotel room, but it also contained clothing from its former occupant. Andriy rummaged through the closet and found some clothes that surprisingly fit him. He put on a sturdy pair of denim jeans, an undershirt, and a large wool sweater. The sweater was roomy enough that he could attach his holster underneath its confines and therefore conceal his pistol. He attached the Bowie knife to an ankle holster. He would have to visibly carry the rifle.

He made his way into the living area and found Fedir playing with Zeus. He paused and soaked up the vision in front of him. A wave of guilt washed over him, as he came to grips with the danger he was putting himself and the boy in. Inhaling a deep breath, he interrupted the scene.

"Are you two ready for our next adventure?" he asked, trying to sound positive.

"Are you sure we can't stay here for a little longer?" Fedir sounded desperate to stay.

"I'm sorry, buddy, but we need to get to Poland. It's the only way we can, hopefully, put a stop to these killings," he sighed.

"What happens to me when the war ends?" Fedir's voice cracked with tears. Andriy hadn't thought that far in the future. He didn't know what would happen to Fedir after the war.

The boy had told him that his family had been wiped out. He didn't know if he had any distant relatives that he could take the boy to. Something protective stirred within Andriy, and he suddenly felt an overwhelming need to comfort the boy and keep him safe. Not just against the war, but the emotional trauma he would surely be subjected to afterwards, as well.

"Would you, um, want to stay with me?" Andriy softly asked.

Fedir's eyes lit up with excitement and joy. Andriy knew it was too soon to ask, but something had come over him, and he wanted to know if the boy felt as close to him as he did to the boy.

"Yes!" he exclaimed, jumping up from the couch and hugging Andriy around his legs. "I would like that very much!"

Andriy was suddenly taken over by his emotions, but he simply patted the boy on his back and said, "Well, that's what we'll do then."

They packed two black nylon satchels that Andriy attached some rope to in order to fabricate backpacks for ease of carrying their essentials. Each backpack contained shelf-stable food, five bottles of water, and a blanket. Andriy knew this wasn't nearly enough provisions, but he couldn't weigh himself down, nor would the boy be able to physically carry everything they needed for the duration of the journey. His hope was that they would find a town or two along the way to replenish what they needed.

In his own backpack, he carried his laptop, extra ammunition for each gun, a first aid kit, and metal bowl to pour water into for Zeus. He also carried the printed results of the research he uncovered from the blister fluids. That was the most precious information, and he knew he needed to keep it safe at all costs.

Andriy looked at his watch. It was close to sunset and his plan had been to travel during the night hours as much as possible. It seemed the safest and the least probable to be seen. Giving one last glance at his surroundings, he checked to see if they had forgotten anything. He knew he was stalling; he didn't want to leave either, but it was something that needed to be done.

"Let's go!" he said sternly, more for himself than for Fedir. They left the office and entered the hallway.

When they reached the main door, he motioned for Fedir and Zeus to stay still. Cautiously, he opened the door. Zeus lifted his nose and sniffed the air, as if he understood that Andriy was looking for any dangers lurking outside. Andriy peeked his head out and scanned the area. Not seeing any immediate danger, they stepped outside. After getting his bearings, they started heading west.

Getting out of the heart of the city had been a little tricky. Even though dusk had set in, he felt they were too visible. He kept the trio weaving in and out of the pulverized buildings, peeking around walls to see if any soldiers were nearby. He could hear distance explosions, but he surmised them to be quite a few miles away. Every so often, they would have to sidestep a body lying in the road or beneath the rubble. He did his best to shield Fedir from the sights, but he knew the boy saw the gruesomeness of ripped apart flesh and blood. Slowly, they made their way away from the carnage. It seemed the further away they traveled, the less ghastly sights they saw. They were headed into farming areas, but not the rural part of the country yet. The danger was still very real here too.

They had been traveling for about five hours, resting only occasionally for a sip of water or a light snack. They had traversed mostly untouched hillsides. The road was scarcely dotted with a burned-out car or military tank. The ground was hard but not so hard that their footsteps could be heard. Andriy couldn't believe his luck not coming across any soldiers along the way. It was as if the entire war was south and east of them. He felt almost happy and that they would indeed make it safely to the border.

Suddenly, Zeus ran ahead to them. Andriy called out for him to stop, but the dog kept going. Zeus stopped about 100 feet ahead of them. He barked once to alert them, and then sat down, his gaze unwavering from a spot on the ground.

The hairs on the back of Andriy's neck stood up in fear. He suddenly realized exactly what training Zeus had had. The dog was a bomb sniffing dog and he just uncovered one directly in their path. Andriy had been so focused on the dog that he didn't see Fedir running towards him until the sight of him reached Andriy's peripheral vision.

Andriy frantically called out for Fedir to stop as he ran after him. The boy was swift footed and was closing in on Zeus faster than Andriy could close the gap. He tore off his backpack thinking he was being weighed down in his stride.

Just as Andriy thought he could reach out and pull Fedir back, Zeus reached the spot he had been concentrating on. Andriy heard a brief yelp before the explosion knocked him and Fedir backwards, hitting the ground hard. The last thing he remembered before he blacked out was seeing the blood on the side of Fedir's head.

CHAPTER EIGHTEEN

Harold Tomlin sat across the table from Alex Sharp. He stared intently at the man before him. So intently, it made Alex squirm slightly in his seat. Tomlin's team had picked him up from Daskin's place within 10 minutes of his failure to kill him. Alex knew how important the assignment had been. The weeks of planning after Crane's research had been discovered. The sheer luck that he had been living in the same neighborhood as Crane as a sleeper agent. Every opportunity had landed within the palms of his hands, and he blew it.

When the team had picked him up, they took him to a hotel room not far from the neighborhood. They left him to clean himself up and dress the bruising bump on the side of his head. The blow from Crane caused a slight tear in his left temple, but the tenderness of the wound was what bothered Alex the most. And the fact that Crane was able to strike a blow to Alex before he could pull the trigger didn't help his ego either. Two hours after arriving at the hotel, the team picked up Alex again and brought him to Tomlin's office. Alex wasn't happy about the impending reprimand.

"I thought I could trust you to clean this mess up, Alexi!" Tomlin growled angrily..

Alex looked up at Tomlin upon hearing his given name used. The daggers in Tomlin's voice irritated Alex.

"Don't call me Alexi!" he snarled back at Tomlin. "I don't like it." Alex liked his new identity.

Although he loved being a Russian spy, the western lifestyle rubbed off on him and he liked the perks of being free. He still loved what he did, but his given name reminded him of the home-life he left behind. A time where he had to prove himself time and time again. Now, he was well adapted to his trade, and he wanted the power he felt he deserved.

"I told you I would clean it up and I still hold myself to that promise." He sat up to face Tomlin eye to eye. "We know where he is. He's been sticking out like a sore thumb with all the purchases he's made with his credit card. It's like he has a beacon attached to his forehead," Alex explained, politely, but with a subtle overtone that was unmistakably dangerous.

Tomlin relaxed ever so slightly at the information, but anger still filled his voice. "When do you plan to finish this?" he inquired.

"I'll get to the hotel early in the morning before he wakes up. It's a remote enough place, I shouldn't bring too much attention." Alex relaxed in his chair, brushing off Tomlin's ire.

"This is your last chance, Alexi!" Tomlin hurled the name at Alex once more, then turned and left the room.

Alex quickly stood up upon Tomlin's exit and grabbed the nearest thing to him; a lowball glass from the bar area of the conference room he had been placed in to meet with Tomlin. Holding the glass in his hand, he lifted his arm with the intent to hurl the object in Tomlin's direction. He stopped himself. With unseen control, he placed the glass back on the table and left the room as well.

Alex swung by the hotel room to grab a few items before he set off to eliminate Crane...again. He picked up his old friend and stared in wonderment at its uselessness. How could his precious gun have betrayed him? With the daunting task before him, he tossed the gun aside onto the bed and picked up a Glock 17. The Glock was nowhere near as elegant and sleek as his Walther P99, but he couldn't trust his friend this time. It pained him to leave the gun behind, but he had a job to do, and mistakes would not be tolerated a second time. He closed the door to the hotel room, got in a car that had been left for him, and headed to the hotel where Crane was peacefully sleeping, unaware that this would be his last sleep. Or so Alex thought.

Alex turned off the headlights and quietly made his way into the parking lot of the hotel. Suddenly, his phone rang. It was Tomlin.

"Yeah," Alex tersely answered the phone.

"He's left," Tomlin curtly replied. "I just got word that Crane left the hotel two hours ago. He's traveling south on I-95. He's almost in Massachusetts." There was a slight panic in his voice.

"Why didn't you know this sooner?" Alex quipped. Anger was rising in his body. More like threatening humiliation of failure.

"I don't know. My informant said something about a power surge that knocked out the transmission. They lost the visual device, but the tracking device is still operational." Tomlin explained quickly. "You need to leave now and follow him. I'll keep you updated on his route, but for now, head south. He's not driving very fast so you should be able to catch up to him soon." Tomlin hung up the phone.

Alex hurriedly pulled the car out of the parking lot and sped towards the interstate. Since it was early in the morning, there was very little traffic to get in his way. He didn't want to draw attention to himself, but he felt comfortable going 15 miles over the posted speed limit. Occasionally, his foot would press harder on the gas pedal, and he had to temper back his speed.

Tomlin updated throughout the trip every 45 minutes. Alex was gaining on Crane. He hoped he would catch up to him somewhere where he could drive him off the road without being noticed. Or, if Crane would stop for a time, he could figure out a way to eliminate him in a way that wouldn't draw attention. Different scenarios played out in Alex's mind on how to kill Crane. He wanted revenge for his own shortcomings of not having terminated him earlier. The failure was a slap in the face, and he wouldn't let it go unpunished.

Tomlin's next update on Crane's location was 10 miles south of Boston. According to the information, he was stopped at a local restaurant. Glancing at the time, Alex guessed that he had stopped to get some breakfast. The thought of food made Alex's stomach growl. He hadn't eaten since early yesterday evening. The restaurant might work to his advantage. He could enter the establishment, locate Crane, quietly finish him off, and grab a bite to eat on his way out. A sinister smile crossed his face as he thought of the idea.

Alex closed in on the location. No further word from Tomlin told him that Crane was still at the restaurant. Alex didn't see Crane's car, but the parking lot was very crowded. *It must be parked around back*, he thought.

He pulled into a parking space, got out and walked into the restaurant. The establishment was packed with early morning customers. The wait staff hurriedly moved from table to table either taking orders or bringing out food. Alex searched the crowd for Crane. He didn't see him. In fact, most of the patrons were elderly men and women. Alex glanced at the specials sign noticing it was senior's breakfast hour.

Alex asked one of the waiters as he passed by where the men's room was. The frazzled teenager nodded his head in the direction of the bathrooms. "Back there," he said, and quickly made his way to a table of hungry gray-haired gentlemen.

Alex opened the door to the bathroom. Checking under the doors of each of the stalls, he realized the bathrooms were empty. Perplexed, he returned to the dining area. He stood in line and waited to be seated. He needed to figure out where Crane was.

He ordered a coffee when a teenage girl with long blonde hair came to his table to take his order. After she left, he pulled out his phone and called Tomlin. "Check your information. He's not here," Alex clipped when Tomlin answered.

"What do you mean he's not there? The tracker is functioning and pinpointed his location to where you are!" Tomlin fired back.

"I'm telling you, he's not here. Something, either your information or your informant, is wrong."

"Let me call you right back. I need to..."

"Wait!" Alex cut Tomlin off mid-sentence. "The car is leaving." Alex hung up the phone and rushed from his seat.

He caught a glimpse of his waitress heading towards his table with his coffee. When she saw him leaving, she huffed and turned back towards the kitchen to throw out the cup.

Alex bolted from the restaurant and sprinted towards the only car leaving the parking lot. Something was off. Looking through the windshield, he noticed two figures in the car: a man and a woman. Neither of which was Crane. The car came to a sudden halt as Alex stepped in front of the car. An elderly couple stared wide-eyed at him. Alex put his hand up, motioning for the car to stop. Bewildered, the couple obeyed. Calmly, he walked up to the driver side as the man rolled his window down.

"Is something wrong?" the gentleman asked.

"Um, no sir. I, uh, I thought I saw you run over a nail. Do you mind if I check your tires for you?" Alex stammered.

"Oh, that would be so kind of you," the man exclaimed. "People are so friendly here," the man said, turning to his wife as Alex made his way to the rear tires.

He felt under the wheel well until his finger brushed up against something solid. It was the tracker. Cursing under his breath, he yanked it from its hiding place and put it in his pocket. He straightened up, plastered a fake smile on his face, and turned back towards the couple.

"I must have been mistaken," he said with all the friendliness he could muster. "I didn't find any nails."

"Well, thank you, son for checking. Here. Get yourself something to eat. On us." The man handed Alex a five-dollar bill, rolled his window up and drove away.

Alex dumbfoundedly stared at the car as it made its way onto the roadway. Deflated, he stuffed the bill into his pocket, got back into his car, and picked up his phone to call Tomlin. It was a conversation he was not looking forward to.

CHAPTER NINETEEN

Dawson piddled around the hotel room for most of the day. He needed a plan once he landed in Poland. If he landed in Poland, he considered the possibility he may not even have a chance to do so. Making the call to Stephanie was only part of the solution. He needed to figure out a way to get in contact with Andriy. He wished he also had a way to get in touch with Sergei should something go wrong. The one-sided communication didn't sit well with his already frayed nerves.

Thinking about Andriy made him remember the conversation with Tomlin. Tomlin had said that Andriy was closing in on the lab where he worked, and he was traveling with a boy. *Andriy must be being tracked too!*

The soldiers must be too far away to get to Andriy, but his luck would run out, Dawson was sure of it. Dawson paced the room trying to figure out how he could warn Andriy if it wasn't already too late. He assumed Andriy didn't know he was being watched, or did he? He could be dead right now for all Dawson knew.

His stomach began to growl. It had been some time since he ate. He decided to go to the motel lobby to see if there was any food to be had. He didn't recall seeing anything last night, but he wasn't in the right frame of mind to observe whether the place had anything to eat or not. Stepping out of his room, he scanned the parking lot. He wondered if he'd be looking over his shoulder for the rest of his life; suspicious of everything and everyone. Not seeing anything concerning, he headed towards the main entrance of the motel.

The bell clanged again as he opened the front door. The place wasn't even modern enough to have sliding entry doors. *That must be wonderful for people ladened down with luggage*, he thought.

There was a new attendant behind the counter. The gruff man from last night had been replaced by a young woman. Dawson guessed her age to be around 25 years old. She had a crisp, clean burgundy polo shirt on with a pair of beige khaki pants. Her hair was pulled up into a bun, but the look didn't take away from her young face. She smiled when Dawson walked up to the counter.

"How can I help you?" she asked pleasantly.

"Um, hi," Dawson started the conversation. "I checked in last night and, uh, I was kind of tired, so I didn't notice if you had a café area, or something."

"Oh, I'm sorry, sir." she said apologetically. "We don't serve any meals here. We don't even have a kitchen. There's a little restaurant up the road called *Claire's* if you're hungry. They serve breakfast, lunch, and dinner." she added.

Dawson glanced at his watch and noticed it was past the time lunch would be served. "Great. Thanks. I'll check it out." He patted the counter and turned to leave.

"Is there anything else I can help you with?" The woman behind the counter lowered her chin and Dawson could have sworn he saw her bat her eyelashes. She was flirting with him!

A small blush crept into Dawson's cheeks. "Uh, no. Thanks. I'm just going to get something to eat." Dawson quickly left the lobby.

Smiling at the flattery, Dawson made his way to his car and headed to the restaurant. The place was clean and the smell of food cooking and being served wafted its way into his nostrils.

"Something smells good," he said to the hostess that greeted him at the entryway.

"That's our early dinner special; Hot open-faced turkey sandwich with gravy." The hostess explained. "How many? Just one?" She asked looking around for any companions.

"Yes, just one," Dawson chuckled wondering why she felt the need to ask if he had anyone else with him since he clearly entered the establishment alone.

"Right this way." She said, grabbing a menu and some silverware. She showed Dawson to a booth alongside the front of the restaurant's windows. She placed the menu and silverware on the table so that Dawson would be sitting with his back to the main entrance. "Will this do?" she asked.

"It's fine," Dawson said, sitting down on the opposite side of the table and moved the menu and silverware over to him. He didn't like the idea of not being able to see who was coming through the front door. He also didn't like the fact that he even had to think about it.

He ordered the special of the day and a soda. He gave the menu back to the waiter once he took his order. Dawson sat staring out the window, watching the patrons coming and going. His mind drifted to what his next move was going to be.

He knew he needed to get to Poland. Stephanie had assured him a place to stay. He briefly wondered if she would join him, but quickly dashed that thought. Once there, he reckoned he would need to get to the Polish Embassy. He was afraid to contact the US Embassy thinking somehow Tomlin would have someone there waiting for him. They would be able to get in contact with the Ukrainian government. He deliberated on how he could convince them that the Russian regime was using chemical warfare against its civilians and soldiers. The evidence Dawson had outlined potentially how the agent was being spread was going to take a lot of convincing.

He imagined that conversation. *So, when you run over, or step on these* altered mushrooms and they release their spores, that's when the chemical is introduced into the immediate atmosphere.

He could hear the skepticism now. However, whether they believed him or not. Whether the evidence convinced them or not was irrelevant. It was a fact. The closer someone was to the release, the more intense the effect. As the laced spores traveled away from the initial discharge, the less effective it was to the human body. It could still pack a punch and leave its victim with blisters, but the side effects could be neutralized with antibiotics.

How am I going to neutralize the initial effects from the burst of spores? Had Andriy come up with any ideas? He thought about these questions as the waiter brought him his lunch. Pushing the thoughts aside, he turned to his food and ate. The one question Dawson didn't ask himself was why wasn't he affected by the spores?

Dawson finished his meal, paid for his tab, and headed back to the motel. His mood had been greatly improved simply by having a full stomach. He pulled into a parking space and got out of the car. His mind, again, quickly scanned his surroundings for any lurking danger. Seeing no one, he walked towards his room. Upon reaching the door, he almost stepped on a flat package lying in front of his room door.

It was a plain white package with an unknown return address. The shipping label attached had his name on it, and the address and room number of the motel. Nothing else gave Dawson a clue as to what its contents may be. He picked up the package and went inside the room.

Dawson's hands were shaking as he held the parcel in his hands. He felt around the package trying to figure out what its contents would be. He felt something hard, but still flexible and guessed it was a passport. Delaying no further, he tore open the package.

As promised by Sergei, the package contained a passport, plane ticket, and some cash. He was surprised to see the cash, but grateful as well. He was running low on money and didn't want to take a risk by using his debit card to get more. Since he hadn't been spotted, he assumed his ploy earlier in switching the tracker and making random purchases worked. What he didn't know was how long before they figured out they had been duped.

He noticed the plane ticket was for a flight tomorrow morning from Boston to Germany. He searched the package for another ticket but came up empty handed. It was just a flight to Germany and nothing else that would get him to Poland. He slumped a little and let out an exasperated sigh. Grateful to be able to get out of the country, but worried about how he was going to get to his final destination. He put the thought in the back of his head for the time being.

He picked up the passport. It was a typical United States passport — dark blue with the golden eagle holding a bundle of arrows and an olive brand emblazoned on the front. The design, as it was known, was said to represent the power of peace. Ironic, Dawson thought, since he was traveling to warn a peaceful country that its invaders were conducting sinister, exploratory chemical warfare on its citizens. The potential fact that the United States was somehow involved only added to the mockery.

The departure flight to Germany was at 6:00 AM. Glancing at his watch, it was already 7:00 PM. The drive would take him at least six hours. *Not much time*, he mused. He could either leave now and crash at some hotel near the airport or he could get some sleep now and wake at a very early hour in the morning.

Feeling too wired to sleep, he decided to pack up what little he had in the motel and leave now. He put his meager belongings in the car and walked over to the main entrance to turn in his room key. The grumpy attendant was back. Dawson didn't care. He wasn't going to see this guy again, so he simply plopped the key on the desk, gave a short "I'm checking out" mumble to the clerk and left. The clerk didn't pay too much attention to Dawson and simply grabbed the key off the countertop, returning his attention to the program on the television.

CHAPTER TWENTY

Dazed and disoriented, Andriy tried to open his eyes. His head was pounding, and he felt like he had just finished a boxing match where he ended up on the mat after five rounds with the world's most elite opponent. Every part of his body hurt. He was alive and that gave him some comfort but the pain he felt wasn't much comfort at all. Recalling the events that put him in this position, he quickly pulled himself up. He winced as his body recoiled from the sharp, sudden movement.

Frantically, he looked over at Fedir and scrambled quickly to his side. The boy was still unconscious. Andriy felt for a pulse with bated breath. Relieved, he found a beat. He scanned Fedir's body looking for any noticeable injuries. He felt his arms, legs, and his torso. Thankfully, the boy was intact and unbroken. Fedir stirred at Andriy's touch.

"What happened?" Fedir managed to ask, still stunned from the explosion.

"I'm not sure, but I think Zeus found a bomb," Andriy softly told him.

"Zeus!" Andriy gently placed the boy back onto the ground. "I'm going to find him. Don't move until I get back," he warned Fedir.

Andriy searched the area with his eyes, looking for any signs of the dog. Turning towards his left, he spotted his limp body. Tears caught in his throat. In a short amount of time, he had grown very fond of Zeus. Now more so given that the dog sacrificed his life to save theirs. With disheartened steps, he walked over to the motionless hero.

Stooping down, he petted the dog ever so gently. He didn't see any visible wounds, but given the dog's posture, he was sure he was dead. How was he going to break the tragic news to Fedir? Andriy remembered the look on the boy's face when Zeus woke him up. The joy the furry bundle had given was simply immeasurable.

He continued to softly pet the dog as he surveyed where the bomb had exploded. Looking at the implosion site, he noticed that there wasn't much debris around it. Not being able to see well, he couldn't distinguish how deep the hole from the bomb had made. It looked deep, but he couldn't be sure. Bombs set by soldiers were usually just under the surface, giving it a bigger and more expansive impact. This one appeared to have been placed too deep below the surface. He needed to get a closer look.

Zeus' leg twitched as Andriy's hand grazed over his paw. Andriy's attention was immediately drawn back to the dog. Incredibly, he realized the dog was still alive. Instant joy spread through Andriy, and he placed his face at the furry neck of the dog. "You're alive!" he exclaimed, as he rubbed his face back and forth in his scruffy fur.

With extreme care, he lifted Zeus into his arms. Zeus gave a small whimper but did not cry out. Andriy carried the dog over to where Fedir was and gently laid him down again. "Fedir! He's alive!" Andriy rejoiced.

Fedir was able to roll onto his side, facing where Andriy had placed Zeus. He reached out his hand and petted the dog. Too emotional to speak, he simply continued to pet the dog, tears of joy streaming down his face.

Andriy sat down next to the pair reveling in the happy scene before him. Then he got up, told Fedir again to remain where he was, and walked over to the inward collapse of the road. As he had suspected, the hole was dug too deep to cause extensive damage to anyone or thing that may have tripped its trigger. Andriy smiled. The Russian soldier that had planted this bomb was probably not properly trained in munitions. Instead of planting the mine at an anti-personnel depth, he must have planted it at an anti-tank depth. Either way, Andriy was grateful for the inadequacy.

Andriy walked back to Fedir and Zeus. Zeus was regaining his strength. Enough so, he was now licking Fedir's face, much to Fedir's delight. He could hear the boy giggling at the wet tongue caressing his cheeks. As he approached, he gathered their belongings that had been strewn about during the explosion. He checked their rations and found most everything still undamaged. He quickly looked at his laptop as well. He didn't want to risk turning it on and draining the battery. A quick survey of the outside of it didn't show anything noticeable, so he placed it back into his backpack.

He wondered if they should try to continue their journey or find shelter for now. Examining their surroundings again, he spotted a small cottage in the near distance a little off the road. "Do you think you can walk?" he asked, turning himself towards Fedir. Fedir looked up from petting the dog.

"I think so." Slowly, Fedir rose to his feet. He felt a little unstable and Andriy quickly steadied him.

"If we can make it to that cottage over there, I think we should rest for a bit." He pointed in the direction of the tiny house.

Fedir nodded his head and tried to bend down to pick up the dog. Swooning slightly at the movement, Andriy quickly swept in and cradled the dog in his arms, supporting Fedir as he did so. "I've got him," he said. Fedir nodded his head appreciatively. Holding the dog and balancing Fedir at the same time, they started to walk.

The trio made their way to the cottage. Their stride was steady, but slow, mostly due to the stiffness and soreness of their recent encounter but also, they were acutely aware that there could be additional mines. They cautiously placed one foot in front of the other, relieved with every step. Their encounter made them skeptical of more mines even though they started walking through the fields, and off the road, towards the cottage.

With both sides apparently using this same road, he didn't want to risk being seen by friend or foe. *Let's just hope no one uses it any time soon*, he thought. He was afraid if spotted by his own countrymen, they would take the boy to a shelter and return Andriy to the war. If spotted by the enemy... he chose not to think of those consequences.

Finally making it to the cottage, Andriy found the front door unlocked. War seemed to make people leave in such a hurry the thought of securing their belongings appeared to be the last thing on their minds. The inside of the place looked to be that of a hunting refuge. An animal skin rug laid in front of a gray stone fireplace. Soot and ashes still peppered its walls and floor. There was a wooden dining table with four wooden chairs surrounding it. The floors themselves were also wood. The inside of the cottage looked like a log cabin even though its exterior was covered with modern day aluminum siding.

There was a small kitchenette area towards the back of the cottage. A refrigerator, a two-burner stove, and cabinets completed the area. Across the kitchen area, but still along the backside of the house, was a four-poster queen sized bed. Heavy quilts adorned the bed, giving comfort to its occupants during the cold winter when hunting season was permissible.

Spotting a well-worn couch, Andriy guided Fedir to sit down. He placed Zeus gently on the animal skin rug and looked around for some firewood. He was hesitant to light a fire as the smoke from the chimney might attract unwelcome guests, but it was getting cold, and they needed heat. He found some wood piled on the side of the fireplace and deftly lit a fire. The warmth of the fire relaxed their muscles, and they sat in silence, each keeping to their own thoughts.

CHAPTER TWENTY-ONE

The six-hour drive to the airport gave Dawson a lot of time to think of his next moves. He was nervous about getting through airport security. He was petrified having his passport scanned at the international travel desk. His mind kept asking if it was all a trap. Sergei sounded sincere on the phone, but Dawson didn't know if it was a trap or not. Russians could be very good at manipulations. Just look at the United States' years of election tampering, he thought. They were always denying involvement but leaving enough evidence to the contrary.

He tried not to think what would happen if he were caught. It depended on who caught him, he guessed. Sergei warned him not to contact Tomlin. *How was Tomlin involved in all this?* He wondered. Tomlin had been at the research meetings. Tomlin had assured ChemComm that it had the backing of the Pentagon and all its resources. Tomlin seemed like one of the good guys. *Could he also be a double agent?* With his high rank within the government and his access to top secret materials, it was a possibility. And the new Russian regime under General Gorsky seemed to have deep pockets; enough to pay Tomlin a sizable amount of money to betray his country. *Anything is possible*, Dawson surmised.

Dawson speculated that Alex was working for the Russians as well. It was the only explanation for Alex trying to kill him. *Could Tomlin be tied to Alex?* If that were true and the Russians were behind all of this – the killings and the chemical warfare, Dawson's life was very much in danger. Much more than he originally thought and much more complicated to get away from. With the endless resources of those wishing him dead, and if the war in Ukraine were to fall into the Russians' favor, he didn't stand a chance.

He was not going to let that happen. Dawson hardened his resolve. His forehead scrounged into a scowl. He was now getting mad. Mad at the audacity of one country trying to destroy another for no reason other than they wanted the land. Dawson cocked his head to the side at the hypocrisy of that thought. Still, Ukraine had established itself as an independent nation and this wasn't the colonization time of the 1700's where more advanced nations were trying to take over any country they deemed weak so they could expand their empire. They deserved peace. Regardless of all that, Russia was in violation of not only the Geneva Convention in using chemical warfare, but in violation of humanitarian rights.

What made Dawson mad the most was the people in his own government siding with these monsters. *What did they hope to gain? Did the United States President know about all this?* Dawson prayed that President Wentworth was in the dark as to what clandestine games were being played behind her back. She would eventually need to be told, but until Dawson could put all the pieces together, he couldn't risk informing her of the crimes. He couldn't trust her; not yet. No. The clear path in getting this all out in the open was to present his research, along with Andriy's, to President Bagan. Let him deal with General Gorsky and if President Wentworth needed to be involved, he could initiate the conversation, Dawson concluded.

He saw his first sign along the roadway revealing that the airport was approaching. He'd be there in about 10 minutes. He shifted in his seat partially from having sat too long in one position and partially because he started to tense up. Mentally, he took inventory of his belongings in his satchel. He didn't have much, only leaving his house with his laptop and keys. He had bought some clothes and the backpack lying on the passenger seat while staying at the hotel.

Nothing stuck out as a potential obstacle in getting through airport security. He needed to come up with an explanation as to why he was going to Germany. He couldn't very well say it was for vacation, given the meager belongings he had with him. He could twist the truth a little and say he was going to surprise his girlfriend with a proposal before she graduated from Heidelberg University where she had been studying to become a nurse. The story seemed plausible, and Dawson decided it was the best he could come up with. If they gauged the truth of his story via his expressions, he would surely pass. All he had to think about was Stephanie, and the story would pass even the most precise lie detector machine.

He was missing Stephanie very much lately. He wasn't sure it was due to loneliness, fear for her safety at the border, or he truly wanted to be by her side. He knew meeting up with her in Poland would be a test of whether they should resume their relationship or not. Deep inside, he hoped they would. With all that had happened recently, his perspective on the value of carpe diem had never been more meaningful than now.

He entered the parking garage for the airport, choosing the long-term location. He didn't know when he'd be returning to the states and didn't want to risk having his car towed if he parked in the daily lot. Grabbing the ticket from the automated kiosk, he entered the garage. There were a lot of cars in the garage, so much so he didn't find a spot until he reached the fourth level. He tucked the car between a pickup truck and a van. He thought that if the people trying to find him ended up at the airport, they'd have a tougher time locating his car. He hated thinking like this. It felt as if he was constantly playing a chess game; needing to think three or four moves in advance. If checkmate came, he would be dead.

Grabbing the passport and plane ticket from his bag, he finally inspected his travel documents. He hadn't even looked at the name he was supposed to be using as an alias. *That wasn't very smart of you*, he grimaced. How was he supposed to pass as...he looked down at the name, *Dawson Crawford*, if he didn't even know the name? He pondered on the name for a minute. It fit. It was close enough to his own name he could remember it and just off enough to hopefully, not raise an alarm to his pursuers.

He found the elevator and pushed the button that would take him to the airport departure level. He was parked only two levels up. The bell rang on his floor and the doors opened to the large terminal area. Travelers were everywhere. Some passengers were sitting on benches, some were waiting in line for security, and some were rushing to their gate in the hopes their flight wouldn't leave without them. He scanned the concourse looking for his airline. He spotted it about 30 feet away. Letting out a deep breath he had subconsciously been holding in, he headed for the counter that had a line of nine passengers waiting to be checked in. He got in line.

He looked at the passengers in front of him. Nothing about any of them stood out. There was a family of three, and two girls mostly likely in their early 20's whispering to each other and giggling as they stared at an attractive man waiting in the next line over to their right. Four businessmen in darker colored suits, obviously strangers to one another since none of them made any attempts at conversation. They stood somewhat slumped as if the years of traveling for one business meeting or another were starting to wear on them. At the end of the line was Dawson.

It didn't take too long before he was being called to the counter.

"Next!" the clerk announced.

Calming his nervousness, Dawson approached the counter and handed the middle-aged woman his ticket.

"Passport, please." she said, holding out her hand, not looking at Dawson. She looked at the hastily glued photo of Dawson that he had attached to the passport and then looked back up at Dawson. Dawson tried to look nonchalant, hiding the sheer panic in his stomach. She looked from the passport to the plane ticket and at Dawson one more time before handing all the documents back to him.

"Concourse C, gate 21," she said curtly. As he turned to leave, he heard her shout again, "Next!"

Walking down Concourse C on his way to gate 21, Dawson only stopped at the restroom and a sundry store to grab a snack and a drink. He didn't have a lot of time before his flight would start to board and he surely did not want to be late. He had almost finished the soda he had bought when the overheard speakers in the waiting room sprang to life and started announcing the seat numbers of passengers allowed on to the plane. He secretly had hoped Sergei would get him a first-class ticket.

The flight to Germany was seven hours long and he would have loved to be able to stretch out his legs. Unfortunately, his seat was smack dab in the middle of the plane. At least he had a window seat so he could look out into the clouds and avoid the inevitable small talk from the occupant next to him. He leaned back into his seat as the rest of the passengers were loaded and the plane took off. Staring blankly at the ground below getting smaller and smaller, he prayed Sergei had a plan for him the next time he saw land.

CHAPTER TWENTY-TWO

"You're not going to believe this," Alex started the conversation, feeling frustrated with the recent turn of events.

"You had better not tell me you lost him again!" Tomlin snarled into the phone.

"Well, I guess there's no point in having this conversation, then," Alex replied, gritting his teeth.

"What the hell happened?" Tomlin was not in the mood for games.

"I'm not sure. He somehow switched the tracker on the car. I found it on some old couple's car with Florida tags. You were the one telling me where he was going. How was I supposed to know he duped us?"

"Damn it!" Alex could hear the frustrated anger in Tomlin's voice. It matched his own.

"There must be someone helping him. He might be book smart, but he isn't trained for this type of diversion," Alex said, searching for some sort of explanation.

"Don't look at my team," Tomlin fired back. "I handpicked each and every one of my men. They're all getting a nice payout from this. They wouldn't do anything to jeopardize their money. Besides...," Tomlin continued. "My men have each been trained in military intelligence and have contacts all over the world. Why would they risk Crane getting away?" he rhetorically asked.

"Then it must be my people, but why?" Alex was thinking out loud. "What would they hope to gain?"

"Whatever and, whoever it is, we need to find out fast. Meet me at the office in five hours. That should give you enough time to get here." Tomlin disconnected the line.

Alex pounded his fist on the steering wheel. The entire mission was falling apart. He did not want to think of the consequences if it failed. His superiors were not as lenient as his American counterparts. He wouldn't have a cushy cell in federal prison, he would either spend the rest of his life in the Siberian labor camps or he would be eliminated. Those were his choices if he didn't find Crane.

He turned his car onto the highway and headed for the office. The office wasn't a typical place where employees sat in cubicles and gathered around the water cooler. It was an abandoned building located in one of the worst neighborhoods in southeast New Jersey. A place where cops didn't venture, and the local gangs knew better than to break into. The high-tech security that surrounded the building was difficult to point out, but precise enough that, once alerted, any intruders were quickly dealt with. Everyone knew it and everyone stayed away.

Tomlin met Alex as he pulled into the building's lot. The two men didn't bother shaking hands and walked into the building together after swiping Tomlin's badge through the door scanner. The overhead lights turned on automatically as they sensed motion. One by one they flickered on, spreading throughout the expanse of the area. The first floor did, in fact, look like a legitimate office. Green fabric walls made a maze of cubicles. *No wonder they called it a cube farm*, Alex presumed.

Each desk mirrored the next, complete with a computer monitor and keyboard, a desk phone, and a calendar on an attached desk strutting out from the side. There were no personal belongings lingering on the desks, no family pictures sitting in frames, no traces of human personalities could be found anywhere in the farm area. It didn't matter to the two men heading for the elevator. The cube farm was intended only for show on the off chance that someone dared to venture inside.

Stepping off the elevator that stopped on the second floor, the men were greeted by the true nature of the office. The computer screens on these desks teemed with life. Thirty monitors were alive with data. Individuals sat in front of these monitors watching or analyzing whatever was shown on their screens. There was talk between the employees, but the tones were hushed as if in a library. Their conversations were strictly about the work they were doing as there was no room for informal chatter.

Alex and Tomlin made their way to the glass enclosed conference room. Once inside, Tomlin pulled the shades so the others would not be able to ascertain their conversation. Too many of them were trained to read lips and this conversation was a need to know only. Alex shut the door as Tomlin finished his task and then both men sat down.

Alex started the conversation, "Who could be helping Crane?"

"Before we tackle that, tell me exactly what happened and how you came to find the tracker." Tomlin looked Alex square in the eye.

Alex explained how he had been given intel that Crane had stopped at a hotel about 45 minutes from his house. He used his debit card to withdraw some cash and used his credit card to make a purchase at a convenience store not far from the hotel. Alex didn't immediately go after Dawson because he received notice from Moscow to hang back for at least a day. Alex didn't question the order. He told Tomlin that the next thing he had heard was from him that Crane was on the move.

"The car had two trackers in it for redundancy. One on the inside and one on the outside. If Crane found the outside tracker and removed it, why wasn't the inside tracker still transmitting?" Tomlin rubbed his face trying to comprehend why there wasn't a signal coming through the inside tracker. "If it had been tampered with, we should have been informed." He turned to Alex.

Alex shrugged his shoulders, "Maybe it just stopped working."

"That can't be. This mission is too important for details like this to be overlooked and not reported." Tomlin squeezed the sides of his temples as if he were trying to massage away a headache. Suddenly, Tomlin's hand fell away from his face and understanding dawned on him.

"The kid Gorsky hired. The one with all the techno-babble intelligence. He was the one monitoring the drone and tracking devices. He's the one helping Crane. He must be!" Tomlin exclaimed.

"If that's true," Alex interrupted, "he could still lead us to Crane."

"Right!" Tomlin agreed. "Let's not report our findings just yet. If we can find out where Crane is heading, maybe we could intercept him."

"We need to get to Moscow, though," Alex said. "We need to get there without being detected. If it really is this kid, we need to get to him before Gorsky does or we'll never get to Crane. Gorsky isn't known to interrogate traitors. He usually just kills them when he finds them," Alex gulped knowing he could suffer the same fate as this kid if he didn't find Crane.

"One good thing that's on our side," Tomlin started, "is that the kid probably doesn't think we're on to him and Gorsky is too busy drumming up more troops for this war. Like the last time, your people are having one hell of a time taking Ukraine." Tomlin grinned at Alex; sarcasm dripped from his words.

Alex looked Tomlin in his eyes, "This isn't my war. My war ended when my countrymen shot my mother and father. I surrendered to the regime long ago. If we don't find Crane, you better hope Gorsky will accept your surrender," Alex scorned.

"We'll find him, don't worry. No thanks to you!" Tomlin countered. "I'll get us a plane to Moscow and then we'll head to the mountains ourselves to see if we can't get some information out of the kid. Be ready to leave within the hour. I'm going down to the cafeteria to grab something to eat. If you can pull your prideful head out of your ass, you can join me." Tomlin rose from the chair and exited the conference room, leaving Alex to fume over his unspoken response.

CHAPTER TWENTY-THREE

After a few minutes of staring into the warm fire, Andriy got up and headed to the restroom. He was looking for some towels so he could wipe the blood off Fedir's head and check to see if his wound needed further attending to. He found a small wash rag and ran some cold water over it. He wet the rag enough to moisten the entire cloth and rang out the excess water. Sitting down next to Fedir, he gently started to wipe his injury.

Fedir winced a little when the cold rag touched his skin but sat still as Andriy cleaned him up. He looked over at Zeus as Andriy wiped away the blood on his temple. He was still overwhelmed and amazed that Zeus was still alive.

"How did Zeus not die in the explosion?" Fedir asked.

"I'm not exactly sure, but I think our enemies are not very well versed in the art of planting explosions," he tried to explain. "When I looked at the blast area, it appeared the bomb was planted too deep. Somehow it exploded from the vibrations of your running to save Zeus." Andriy regretted the words as soon as they left his lips.

"I'm sorry, Fedir," he stammered. "I didn't mean to say it like that. You didn't know. I didn't know either. It was probably some fluke wire that was sensitive to your footsteps. It was a good thing that you were running. We would never have known that there were bombs planted." He tried to sound encouraging. It wasn't working.

"It's all my fault," Fedir muttered as he started to cry.

"No, no. It's not. Don't blame yourself for any of this," Andriy soothed. "This war is not your fault. It's not your parents' fault. It's not your teacher's fault. It isn't even President Bagan's fault. All of this is General Gorsky's fault."

"Do you think we can get someone to stop all this killing?" Fedir inquired.

"I do. And that's why we're going to Poland. I have information to relay to President Bagan. The soldiers, not all of them I assume, under General Gorsky's command are doing very bad things to our people. He's going to stop them," Andriy explained.

Still feeling guilty from Andriy's recount of the explosion, Fedir looked to him. "Do you think we'll make it to the border alive?" His softly spoken question made Andriy well up. He folded Fedir in his arms and gently rocked him.

"Of course, we will," he soothed. "We've got Zeus looking after us. We'll make it, I'm positive."

Fedir pulled himself away from Andriy and strolled over to where Zeus had been quietly lying. He gently patted his fur. Zeus raised his head and looked at Fedir. Gingerly, he rose from his resting spot and started to lick Fedir's face as to reassure him of Andriy's spoken words.

Fedir delicately pushed at different parts of Zeus' body. The dog didn't wince. "I think he's going to be okay," Fedir smiled at Andriy.

"I think you're right." He got up and joined the boy. He checked Zeus for any broken legs. He looked at his eyes looking for any broken blood vessels in the whites of his eyes. He also put his fingers on his chest feeling for his heartbeat. "He seems pretty good," Andriy said. "I don't feel anything broken. He's probably very sore, but he's a tough little fellow, I'll give him that." He patted the dog's head lightly. "Why don't I see if I can find us something to eat and we'll rest here for the night so everyone has a little time to heal?" Andriy offered, getting up and he headed towards the kitchen.

"I like that idea," Fedir said, smiling, as he continued to pet Zeus.

Andriy got up and walked into the kitchenette area in search of food. The space had a few wooden cabinets above and below the sink and stove areas. Pulling the handle on each of the cabinets, he found a few staple products most Ukrainian homes contained. There wasn't much. It seems the occupants of the tiny house were either only using the place for rest from hunting or the economy had hit them as much as it did everyone else, and supplies were scarce. He found a partially opened jar of peanut butter, and a box of instant mashed potatoes. Andriy paused as he shook the box. Most Ukrainians dared not use instant mashed potatoes as they always prepared fresh cooked meals; however, given the economy, some were lucky just to get that.

He opened the refrigerator and had better luck. He found potatoes, carrots, unsnapped peas, and eggs. He sniffed and squeezed the vegetables to make sure they were still edible. The eggs were a little more difficult to tell. He'd have to crack them open to inspect their freshness. He also found an open jar of pickles and a jar of mayonnaise among some other partially used containers. He had the ingredients to make Olivye. He hadn't had a traditional meal in quite some time, and he thought it a great idea for him and Fedir to have one tonight.

It didn't take long for Andriy to whip the ingredients to make the dish. It was quite a simple dish to execute. Once finished, he called Fedir over to the table.

"Have a seat, young man. I have a surprise for you! "he exclaimed as he presented the dish in a bowl in front of Fedir.

Fedir's eye lit up at the meal in front of him and started to eat.

"Ah, hold on there, buddy. I think we need to say a little prayer from coming out of that situation relatively unhurt." Andriy sat down and folded his hands to say a grateful prayer that the three of them were still alive. He added a quick request that they'd get to the border safely from here on out and then nodded to Fedir that he could eat.

The two of them sat in silence with the only sound being that of the silverware hitting the bowl to scrape up the contents of the Olivye. Andriy smiled at his ability to recall the recipe and create the dish rather well. It was a good, hearty meal and something he nor Fedir had had in a few days, if not longer. Zeus patiently stared up at the duo while they devoured their meal. As they were finishing up, he gave a slight whine indicating that he, too, was hungry. Andriy looked down at his sad eyes, silently begging to be fed as well.

"Hang on, boy. I'll get you something to eat, too." Andriy got up from the table and searched the cabinets again for something suitable. He found a can of tuna fish behind the peanut butter. It wasn't much, but there wasn't much in the cabinets to begin with. He opened the can and decided whether to drain the juice. He didn't. Might as well give the dog all the nutrients he could get. Pouring the entire contents into a bowl, he lowered it to the floor. Zeus didn't move. Puzzled by his lack of enthusiasm, Andriy told him to go ahead and eat. Zeus sprung from his seated position and politely ate the food. Andriy smiled at the pooch for having such good manners.

"You're such a good boy!" he said as he watched Zeus eat.

Looking back over to Fedir, Andriy watched him finish his meal. "We're going to have to keep moving, you know?"

Fedir scooped the rest of the food into his mouth and nodded. "I know," he said in between chews.

"We can rest for a little while first. I think we all could use a quick nap before we head out." Andriy made his way back into the living area and stoked the fire. He added two more logs gauging the time it would take for them to burn out. He didn't want to stay much past then. He was already anxious enough that they had had to make this detour in the first place.

The three of them settled in the living room as best they could given the sparse amount of furniture. Zeus settled in front of the fireplace, Andriy took the worn recliner and Fedir sprawled out on the couch. It wasn't long before they all were fast asleep in the warm glow of the fire.

Andriy was the first to wake up. Checking his watch, he had only slept 20 minutes. The brief slumber had done an amazing job of rejuvenating him. He got up quietly from the chair. He didn't want to wake the rest up yet. Zeus raised his head. Not noticing anything out of the ordinary, he laid it back down.

Andriy walked to the back of the house and peaked out the door's window. He slowly turned the handle of the door and opened it. His eyes surveyed the surroundings looking for any signs of danger. He could hear gunfire in the far distance but gleaned it wasn't close enough to cause concern. He could barely make out a buzzing sound that seemed to be getting closer. Looking to the skies where the sound was coming from, he realized it was a jet heading towards the city. He didn't think the pilot would be able to see him from such a great distance, but he stood back into the shadows of the door frame for good measure anyway.

After the jet flew over, he stepped out onto the porch. He noticed a tarp covering a rather large object. He decided to further inspect it. Walking towards it, he could make out the shape of a car. His heart raced with excitement as he pulled back the tarp. Underneath was a newer model Chevrolet sedan. He gave the car a once over. There were tiny spots of rust here and there but nothing to suggest that the car had been sitting for more than a month. The windows were dingy, but not broken. He checked the door handles only to find them locked. Andriy wondered if the house occupants left the keys.

Trotting back to the house, he whisked through the back door as quietly as he could in his eagerness to find the keys. Upon entering the house, he found Fedir and Zeus awake. He walked hurriedly over to Fedir and sat down on the couch.

"I think I may have found transportation!" he exclaimed. "There's a car out back but it's locked. Do you think you can help me search for the keys?"

Fedir sprung from the couch, happy to help. Andriy's elation was contagious. The pair searched the living room and kitchen. They opened the cabinets in the kitchen and tossed the cushions from the furniture in the living room. Coming up empty-handed, they stared at each other as if one of them would suddenly produce the keys.

Andriy scanned the rooms looking for any hiding places the owners would have placed the keys. His eyes came to rest on the mantle of the fireplace. He walked over to the mantle and placed his hand on a tiny, wooden music box. *What a Moonlit Night* sprung from the music box's internal workings. It was a Ukrainian folk song about a boy who invites a girl into the night to spend time with him. The tune caught Andriy off guard and he stood there, listening to the notes.

Shaking his head to clear the memories of his parents dancing to the old folk song, Andriy reached into the box. Inside were the keys to the car. He almost jumped with joy at finding them. He raced back outside with Fedir in tow. Zeus had also followed them, both drawn to the enthusiasm of the moment.

Andriy unlocked the car and got behind the wheel. He inserted the key and said a little prayer. At first, the car's ignition didn't turn over. He turned the key back to the starting position and tried again. This time, the engine turned over. He stopped himself short of screaming out in glee. He got out of the car and motioned for Fedir to come with him back into the house.

"We need to get our things out of the house," he reminded Fedir.

They gathered the meager belongings, strapping backpacks back in place. They put their dishes in the sink out of respect for the owners though they doubted the occupants would return. Andriy made several trips from the kitchen to the fire with bowls full of water. He surely didn't want to leave embers burning.

Once everything was back in its place and the pair had all their necessities, they left the house and got into the car. The time they had spent in the house gave the car enough time to warm up. Zeus and Fedir got into the backseat and settled in. Andriy pulled the car onto the gravel roadway keeping it dead center. He didn't need another bomb going off. He estimated he could make the Polish border by daybreak. Pure adrenaline was rushing through his veins now. He gave himself a glimmer of hope.

CHAPTER TWENTY-FOUR

Stephanie returned to work the next morning to find the entire area bustling with urgency and a touch of apprehension. Finding Cara, she asked what was going on.

"I'm not sure," Cara began. "I thought the surge of contaminated soldiers and civilians was over." Upon hearing Cara use the word 'contaminated', Stephanie knew she was speaking of the patients with the mysterious blisters.

"What makes you think it's not over?" Stephanie questioned with unnerving anticipation of the answer.

"Look around you," Cara pointed out. "There's been a surge of new patients. Hundreds of them. All of them were infected with blisters. All of them in varying degrees of severity. Some of them are already dead." Her voice was on the fringe of panic.

Stephanie looked around and concentrated on all the activity. Medics were sprinting between tents carrying medical supplies and hazmat gear. Patients could be heard in the different tents with different cries for help. Some were simply moaning while others were out and out screams of pain. Some tents were deathly quiet.

Summoning up whatever courage she could, Stephanie headed towards the tent with the loudest commotion. Cara grabbed her arm before she could get too far.

"What are you doing?" Her voice was full of alarm.

"I'm going to help. What do you think I'm doing?" Stephanie looked at her friend with confusion.

"Not like that you're not!" Cara pushed Stephanie towards the medical tents. "You need to gear up first."

Stephanie and Cara entered the chaotic medical tent looking for the supplies they would need to assist with the influx of patients. They waited for a minute or two for someone to help them get their gear. It was apparent that the medics were too busy loading up their own supplies to worry about the two volunteers.

Cara moved first. She headed over to the supply cabinet to get gloves and face shields. Stephanie took her cue and headed over to the other storage area to grab full hazmat suits. She silently prayed that the thinly plastic-coated, paper outfits would protect her. Her mind flashed back to the sickness she had overcome while barely exposed to the mysterious toxin emulating from the sick patients. She surely didn't want to go through that again, but she most definitely didn't want to go through anything worse.

Coming back together with the needed protection, Stephanie and Cara slipped the attire on over the regular clothes. Once fully geared up, they both looked like they were headed to a radiation laboratory instead of a field hospital. They exited the tent and started towards the other tents. Stephanie to the one she initially was headed for and Cara to the silent tent. Each of them unaware of what they would find once inside, but each of them dedicated enough to go anyway.

Pure determination drove Stephanie to the tent and as she stepped inside, she was still unprepared for what she saw. All thirty-six of the makeshift beds were filled with patients. Judging by what clothing was left on them, she noticed more than half of the patients were soldiers and the rest were civilians. Gauze bandages scattered the floors stained with brown fluids. The bare chests of the victims were covered in the familiar blister-clusters as well as their necks. Some were gasping for air while others stared off into the void, mouths open with foam slowly flowing onto the bed sheets. The smell was not muted by the suit Stephanie was wearing. The putrid air filled her nostrils and her stomach started to revolt from the odor.

Nurses scrambled between patients, checking vital signs, checking pupils, wiping the oozing blisters, and pulling the sheets over those they could no longer help.

"Nurse! Get over here!" a doctor shouted, jolting Stephanie from her trance. She quickly ran in the direction of the voice.

Reaching the bed, she looked down into the face of a soldier that could not have been more than twenty years old. He was covered in blisters. The fluid had burst from its base and the other nurses had done their best to clean him up. His chest and neck were still stained from the brown fluid and the skin around the blisters was still hanging where they had been lanced open. The soldier's breath was shallow, and his eyes stared blankly at her. His eyes barely pleading as life slowly left his body. He gave one small shutter, and then he was still.

Stephanie gently touched the doctor's arm, guiding it away as she grabbed the end of the sheet and pulled it over the dead man's face. She and the doctor let out a resigned sigh as they looked at each other and then moved to the next patient. Medics quietly came in behind the two as they moved away from the bed and removed the body, only to have another patient take its place.

Stephanie lost track of time as she went from patient to patient trying to save them. Some were beyond her capabilities, but others were able to be patched up and sent to another tent for recovery. She made a mental note as to what condition a patient was in and what their prognosis was. The evidence she was able to ascertain was that a patient with the least number of blisters tended to live, while those with more, didn't. It also appeared that those who were dressed in the tell-tale agricultural clothes of rural Ukraine seemed to be less afflicted. This information, she felt, was important and she would make sure if she got the chance to talk to Dawson again, she would pass along what she had learned.

Caught up in her thoughts, she barely heard Cara call her name.

"Hey, Stephanie!" she touched her shoulder to get her attention.

"Oh, sorry. I was just thinking about why some patients were sicker than others," she said as she turned to Cara.

"Yeah, I noticed that the ones I saw, the ones who were already dead." She closed her eyes trying to shut out the images of the tent she had spent her entire day in. "They were covered almost from head to toe in blisters. What do you think it means?"

"I'm not sure," Stephanie stated. "Why don't we go get something to eat. Maybe we could compare notes to what we saw and see if there is any connection. I have a feeling there is something there, but I'm not exactly sure what 'it' is." Stephanie and Cara started walking to the chow tent.

"I know you told me Dawson was coming. Do you think he will know what to do with the information?" Cara asked.

"I'm sure he'll figure it out. He's good at solving these kinds of problems." Stephanie became worried about Dawson again. The whole situation promised to be a complicated one at best, and a dangerous one at the worst. Dawson was in trouble. Enough trouble to come here to Poland. Soldiers and civilians were coming to the border with a mysterious illness. Someone was keeping it out of the press, too. *Were the Russians blocking transmissions to the States?*

Surely, some journalist could get through to let the world know what was going on. The pieces of the puzzle that were coming together in Stephanie's mind were not fitting nicely together and once the puzzle was complete, she feared that all of them were going to be fighting for their lives. She didn't realize just how very close she was to the truth.

CHAPTER TWENTY-FIVE

At the sound of the captain's voice announcing the plane's preparation for descent into Munich International Airport, Dawson woke with a start. He was surprised he had been able to fall asleep. He was more surprised that he slept the entire flight. The passenger next to him gave him a smile as his mind came into focus.

"Good morning," he said cheerfully.

Dawson cleared his throat and wiped his hand over his eyes and face. "Good morning," he returned, not as cheerful.

He silently wished that he had woken up before the plane started descending. What he wouldn't give for a cup of coffee right now. He stretched his body as much as he could in the confines of his seat, trying to smooth out the stiffness of his muscles from being motionless and cramped for six hours.

When he heard the wheels of the plane disengage from underneath the plane's landing panels, adrenaline shot through Dawson's veins. He didn't want to alarm his seat mate, so he tried to calm his nerves. The scenarios of being captured sped through his mind. He could feel sweat starting to pool on his upper lip. Calm yourself! His mind screamed at him.

"Don't like landing?" the guy next to him innocently asked, noticing the moisture on Dawson's lip.

"Uh, no. No. I don't like landing," he lied as he wiped the evidence away.

"Don't worry, it'll be over soon, and you'll be safe on the ground," he assured Dawson.

"Yeah. Safe. Thanks." Dawson turned his focus forward giving the man next to him the impression he was simply nervous about touching down. Dawson used the distraction to take slow, deep breaths. His heart rate steadily lowered. He needed to have a clear head for when he exited the plane. He had no idea what his next move was going to be, and he was at the total mercy of Sergei to come through. He didn't like relying on someone else for his safety, but that is where he found himself now.

With a bump and the momentary force of braking, the plane landed and began to taxi to their gate. The Munich airport was busy with planes from all over touching down or taking off. Dawson glanced out the window and saw the activity. Planes from different countries could be seen all over. A white plane with the letters LOT caught his eye. The Polish Airline. Well, at least there was a possibility of getting out of here after all, he concluded.

The plane came to a complete stop and the captain finally turned off the seatbelt light. Dawson stood up and opened the overhead compartment that held his meager belongings. He gave a slight nod to the man who had been seated next to him and made his way off the plane.

Dawson leisurely walked down the jetway to the terminal. Other passengers swept past him, seemingly in a greater hurry than he was to get to their destination. He did not share in their excitement. Hell, he didn't even know what his next destination was.

Spilling out into the terminal with the rest of the people, Dawson moved to the side of the gate entrance to pause and gather his thoughts. He looked around at the small shops inside the airport. There was a magazine store for passengers wanting something to read on their long flight. A couple of food establishments to provide for those who wanted something more than the meal that was given on the plane. Dawson spied a bar not too far from where he was standing. *This looks like the perfect place to begin*, he thought.

As he started walking towards the bar, looking forward to a nice whiskey, he was suddenly patted on his right shoulder. Spinning around, he came face to face with a man who looked to be in his early thirties. He was taller than Dawson, but only by a few inches. He was wearing baggy pants and a heather-grey sweatshirt that said *Peace* across the front.

"Mr. Crane?" he hesitated. His voice carried a slight accent that Dawson immediately placed as Russian. Panic immediately set in.

Dawson started to pull away from the man, but his hand gripped his shoulder firmly.

"I mean you no harm," he whispered close to Dawson. "Sergei sent me." The man relaxed his grip and held out his hand indicating he wanted to shake Dawson's hand.

Dawson took his hand and shook it. "Why don't we get a drink?" the man suggested. "I'm Boris, by the way."

Still in shock, Dawson simply said, "Okay." The pair walked towards the bar.

Finding a booth close to the back of the bar, the two sat down. A waiter appeared and asked what they would like to drink. Dawson ordered a whiskey, neat while Boris ordered a pale German ale. Dawson started the conversation after the waiter took their order.

"How do you know Sergei?" Dawson asked, still nervous at Boris' sudden and unexpected appearance. He didn't know what to expect but having someone approach him in the airport wasn't what he anticipated.

"Sergei is my brother," Boris replied matter-of-factly. "He has told me what he suspects is going on with the war in Ukraine and what our government is trying to do. We are sympathizers to the Ukrainians. I know Sergei has told you about our family, our sister and her family, more precisely."

"Yes. He mentioned your nieces and that Sergei is their godfather,"

Dawson added.

"Those girls are very precious to Sergei and me. Neither one of us could live with ourselves if something happened to them. The war is getting very close to where they live now. And, with the information that Sergei has shared with me, it looks like they're in more danger than just from bombs and gunfire."

"What other details do you know about what is happening in the war?" Dawson pried.

"There appears to be some sort of chemical infecting the soldiers around major cities in Ukraine. Unfortunately, it's not just the soldiers that are being targeted. It appears there have been some civilian casualties as well. We're hearing reports from the Polish borders to where the refugees and injured soldiers are traveling that there are many people afflicted with blisters filled with a curious brown liquid. Is that what you've discovered?" Boris looked to Dawson for answers.

"Yes. I have a counterpart, so to speak, who is a Ukrainian soldier, who informed me of this strange condition he discovered on bodies in the streets of the cities. From I what I know of him, he's probably on his way to the Polish border in hopes of getting the information to President Bagan. We're both hoping that President Bagan can convince our President Wentworth to act in Ukraine's best interest and put a stop to it. We believe that General Gorsky and his henchmen are behind all this." Dawson sat back in the booth as the waiter appeared with their drinks. He took a long sip of the soothing liquid, letting the burn warm his throat and relax his muscles.

"It wouldn't surprise me that Gorsky is behind this. He had the entire Russian population fooled when he took power after his coup over his predecessor." Boris, too, paused to take a swig of his ale.

"He had everyone thinking that he could bring peace to our borders and strengthen the bond with the neighboring countries. He really pulled the wool over our eyes, as you Americans say." Smiling at the idiom.

"So, what's the plan now?" Dawson waited for Boris to finish his sipping his ale.

"We get you to Poland," Boris stated bluntly.

"And how exactly do we do that?" Dawson was beginning to lose his patience, but he kept it in check knowing it was coming from the combination of tiredness and utter anticipation.

"I fly us to Poland. We leave in two hours." Boris gulped down the rest of his beer, smiling at Dawson.

CHAPTER TWENTY-SIX

Tomlin and Alex landed at Domodedovo International Airport around 10:00 AM, Moscow time. The airport was further away than the other two international airports. It was chosen precisely to keep the attention away from Tomlin. His physique made him stand out like a sore thumb. Americans were not highly welcomed in Moscow given the country's stance on supporting Ukraine. Tomlin, when making the arrangements, secured a flight that would not taxi to the terminal upon arrival.

A man dressed in a black suit inconspicuously greeted them as they descended the plane's step onto the runway. He shook both hands of the men and guided them to a black Mercedes sedan waiting for them. The air was chilly even with the sun shining, and Alex was thankful that the car had been running while it waited for the plane. Tomlin and Alex made their way to the back seats of the warm car while the unidentified man got into the driver's seat. Once everyone was situated, he turned to the pair.

"Good morning, gentlemen. My name is Colonel Nicoli Stalin." Holding up a hand, he continued. "Before you ask, yes, I am a descendant of Joseph Stalin. He was my great-great-grandfather. I am one of the very few of his descendants that kept his surname." Alex could see the Colonel ever so slightly puff out his chest.

"I am taking you, under General Gorsky's orders, to the bunker in Belarus. Where, I understand, there is an issue with one of our analysts, no? Or was it that he uncovered some, how do you say, deficiencies in your plan?" He stared directly at Tomlin.

Tomlin gave a slight gulp, wondering how the General found out about his suspicions. Waving off the thought because it didn't matter, General Gorsky either knew, or knew how to find out about, everything. Tomlin also realized that General Gorsky would also know that Alex had lost Crane. That thought gave him some trepidation.

"Yes. That is correct." Cutting the Colonel off from any further taunting. Tomlin tried to sound confident, maybe a little defiant too. The Colonel gave a small, smug grin and turned back around in his seat.

The drive to the bunker was quiet. Neither the passengers nor the driver were interested in conversation. The situation didn't warrant small talk, so each man kept their thoughts to themselves.

Tomlin thought about what he would say to General Gorsky. He stood to lose a lot of money if he couldn't secure Crane or Koval before they could reach each other. The evidence the two could present to President Bagan or President Wentworth would ruin Gorsky's hold on the country and, if tied to him, ruin Tomlin as well. His dream of shedding his government job and basking on one of the many islands in the Caribbean would be gone, as well as the million-dollar payment that would set him up for life.

He didn't doubt for a minute that Gorsky would turn on him and report his activities to the US Federal authorities the second suspicion fell on him, and Tomlin would end up in a federal prison with only an hour of sunshine a day, unless called to work. Federal prisons weren't the country club institutions that they used to be. These days, inmates were worked so hard. They were used for manual labor in road construction, trash clean up, and occasionally, grave digging. It was a fate Tomlin did not want to consider. Not to mention the humiliation his conviction would bring to his wife and daughter.

Tomlin thought of his daughter, Lynnie. She had just turned 18 and was getting ready to graduate from high school in a few months. She was the only joy left in his loveless marriage. Lynette, his wife, was always badgering him, telling him how he should use his influence to catapult his career and get into politics. Tomlin hated politics. Lynette wanted the spotlight and attention a high cabinet position would bring her. Lynnie had been accepted into an Ivy League school. Well, Tomlin had bought her admission to the school. He had taken out a loan against his house knowing it would be paid back with the money Gorsky promised him. Lynnie was the apple of Tomlin's eye. A smile crossed his face when he thought of her. The smile caught Alex's attention.

"What are you so happy about?" he seethed through clenched teeth at Tomlin. "Do you think this is funny?"

Tomlin whipped his head to Alex. "We wouldn't be here if you had done your job!" His voice was low, but Alex heard the irritation in it.

Tomlin promptly turned his gaze back to the road ahead. The two said nothing further until they reached the bunker.

The bunker entrance was surrounded by a tall, thick-metal fence guarded by two soldiers armed with assault-style weapons hanging on their shoulders and pistols strapped to their waists. They stepped in front of the main gate as the car approached, reaching for their rifles. One menacing looking soldier approached the driver's side holding his hand up for the car to stop.

Colonel Stalin lowered the window, his credentials in hand. The soldier studied the identification and then peered into the car at Tomlin and Alex. His emotionless eyes gave the passengers a once over and then he stood up, waving the vehicle through the gate.

The car slowly rolled through the gate and towards the façade of a medical building; mirrored windows brightly reflecting the sun.

The Colonel rested the car just outside another door labeled "Lab One". The trio exited the car each stretching a little from the ride and straightening their clothing.

"Follow me," the Colonel instructed. Tomlin and Alex fell in line behind him as he opened the door.

Lab One was teeming with people and monitors. Overhead lighting shone down on about twenty workers each intently watching different scenes on their screens. It was clear that this room held the analysts that were spying on various situations in Ukraine. One particular space caught Alex's attention. Not because of the pictures that were being broadcast, but because the seat was empty.

Alex realized his companions had continued through the work area and were headed to what appeared to be a conference room. He could make out a long table and swivel chairs surrounding it. He started to relax. However, the Colonel did not go into the conference room, rather he opened a door that was to the left of it. Alex didn't get a glimpse of where they were headed until they were almost upon the door. His face fell when he realized what it was. It was a soundproof interrogation room, and it was already occupied.

Sergei sat slumped in a chair. His hair was matted with blood and a large gash could be seen directly above his right ear. His eyes were swollen shut, covered in blood and bruises. His arms hung limply over the arm of the chair, dripping crimson liquid from his fingertips onto the tile floor beneath them. Alex thought the man was dead until he saw a minute twitch of his hands and the shallow breathing from the rise and fall of his chest. Alex was concentrating so hard on the poor soul hanging on for life in the chair that he didn't see the figure in the shadows of the corner of the room until he stepped into the light.

General Gorsky's frame came into view and Alex visibly took a step backwards. The General was a very large man. Not so much in girth but in bulk. He stood an even six-feet tall. He had black hair that was slicked back on top and shaved on the side. A Marine cut, but longer. His face was encased in a dark beard that had been neatly cut and shaved. His short sleeve, green military t-shirt was snug but not tight, accentuating toned muscles in his upper arms and chest. His waist was trim affirming his well-known exercise routine. The only thing that seemed to be out of place on the General was his hands. They were covered in blood. Alex could only assume that the General himself had delivered the punishment to the man collapsed in the seat beside him.

Grabbing a towel that had been sitting on the table, the general wiped his hands as he addressed his spectators.

"Good afternoon, gentlemen." Checking his watch to verify the time of day. His voice was deep but soft, almost hushed. It was not to be mistaken for tenderness.

Tomlin and Alex nodded their heads in unison to the greeting. Colonel Stalin took his cue. He clicked his heels at attention, slightly bowed to the general, and then discreetly exited the room. As the door soundlessly shut, the general motioned for the men to sit.

"Take a seat, gentlemen. Please," he instructed. Once everyone was seated, he stretched his legs out in front of him, absently wiping his hands, and resumed the conversation. "Now, which one of you is to blame for losing our Mr. Crane?" The question hung in the air. Tomlin and Alex looked desperately at one another. The answer would dictate the outcome of the life or death of the person who responded first.

CHAPTER TWENTY-SEVEN

Andriy drove the car under the cover of night. He stopped only once for fuel. Lucky for him, the attendant paid him no mind as he paid for the gas and a little extra for his silence. Andriy could bet he wasn't the first able-bodied male the attendant sold his gas to. Sheer panic, fear, and unexpected optimism had kept him going. He didn't know why he felt the latter. Maybe because the closer they got to the border without incident, the more confident he became. Whatever it was, he was grateful to be alive and nearing safety.

He wondered what kind of questioning they would be subject to. Though he was dressed in civilian clothes, he still carried his military weapons. He could ditch the weapons and try to blend in with the rest of the refugees. He'd have to explain the car. On the other hand, he could ditch the car a mile or so from the border and they could walk. He sighed at the thought of walking again. When this war was over, he decided he would lay in bed for a month, only to get out of it to take care of nature and eat.

He guessed they were about 5 miles from the border when he noticed a few families walking on the road. He beeped the horn warning them to move aside. Passing the travelers, he waved and continued driving. About a mile later, there were more people. A lot more. Too many to navigate the car through. It was then that Andriy realized that they too, were going to have to walk.

Andriy pulled the car to the side of the road. At first, he was a little hesitant to do so given the experience he had had. Nevertheless, he brought the car to a stop and put it into park, turning the ignition off. He turned to his passengers in the back seat and gently nudged Fedir awake.

Fedir sat up, groggy. "Where are we?" he mumbled trying to wipe the sleep from his eyes.

"We're almost there, buddy." Andriy tousled the boy's hair. Zeus yipped with muted excitement. Andriy gave the dog a quick pat on the head.

Everyone got out of the car. Andriy decided against leaving his weapons for the time being. He hoisted the strap of his rifle onto his shoulders and secured the pistol in his side holster. He opened the door for Fedir and Zeus to get out and shut it behind them once they exited the vehicle. They walked over to the crowds of migrants and joined in.

Some people stared at Andriy when they first joined the travelers. Some nodded their heads in greeting, while others simply kept their gazes forward. There was little talking. In fact, it seemed that everyone simply shared an unspoken pact of silence.

Looking around at the faces of his fellow companions, Andriy noticed that the crowd was full of mostly women and children. Scattered here and there were the elderly; those too old to be recruited for fighting. The Ukrainians valued all people and much more so the elderly. They were old, and therefore their legacies were ones that were held in reverence. The government and its citizens all took part in caring for the elderly. It was something of which Andriy was proud.

Spotting one specific elderly couple, Andriy made his way over to them. He unzipped his backpack while still juggling it on his shoulders. He pulled out a bottle of water he had brought from the lab. He hadn't needed it since leaving the lab and it looked as if this couple did.

Handing them the bottle, he said, "Here. Take this. You look like you could use something to drink."

The man took the bottle from Andriy and handed it to his wife to take the first drink. Once finished, she handed the bottle back and the man finished drinking the remains of the water.

"Thank you," he said gratefully. "We have been traveling for two days. We left our homes in such a hurry, we didn't think to pack anything but some clothes."

"Where are you coming from?" Andriy inquired.

"Lviv. The Russians were just coming into the area. We wanted to stay, but with what we had been hearing in the news, we thought it best to leave when we could before they started killing civilians." The man looked down at the ground, sorrow stirred in his voice.

"I'm so sorry." It was all Andriy could think of saying.

He thought about his research and gently pried the man for more information. "Did you notice anything, um, unusual when you were leaving."

The man looked up at Andriy and then to his wife. She barely nodded her head at her husband. The man stepped closer to Andriy as if to tell him a secret.

"There were drones," he whispered in Andriy's ear.

Moving his head away from the man's lips, Andriy looked at him, confused. "Drones?" he repeated.

"Yes. Lots of them. Tiny drones. They were in the fields. Not the wheat fields, but the fields that were left to regrow the nutrients that the wheat strips from the land. It was grassy and full of mushrooms. You know how they grow in the climate this time of year," he said off-handedly.

Andriy's eyes grew wide as the man told him what he had seen. *Drones!* Andriy's mind flashed with all the puzzle pieces of his research. *That's how the Russians were infecting the mushrooms. Drones! That was the missing piece!* Somehow, they were able to maneuver the drones over the mushrooms. They must have used some type of spraying mechanism to cover the mushrooms with the ZMD.

Andriy thanked the man and his wife for the information and hurried away from them to catch up to Fedir who had been casually strolling with the pace of the crowd, and Zeus entertaining the other children as they continued their journey. The couple gave him an odd look as he rushed away, thinking him a little rude for his hasty departure.

"Fedir. We need to hurry!" Andriy's speedy announcement caught Fedir by surprise. Instantly, he was full of dread.

"What's happened?" he questioned.

"I know how the Russians are making people sick," he told Fedir. "We've got to get to the border quickly. Do you think you can walk faster without bringing on any undue attention?"

"We could play fetch with Zeus," he offered. "I'll ask one of the other kids if they have a ball Zeus could play with. I can toss it to him and then hurry after him once he catches it."

"That's brilliant!" Andriy almost shouted at the sheer genius of the boy's idea.

It didn't take long for Fedir to find a ball for Zeus. To onlookers, the game of fetch was a welcomed distraction from the monotony of the walk. They watched as Fedir threw the ball to Zeus and he would run after it. Feigning merriment, Fedir and Andriy would chase after him all the while closing the distance to the border.

It didn't take them long to reach the border. Their game of fetch had allowed them to make the trek in only 2 hours. Andriy and Fedir fell in line with those waiting to be checked through the gate. Andriy had completely forgotten about his rifle until it drew the attention of one of the border guards.

"You!" He pointed at Andriy, placing his hand on his side pistol. "Hands up!"

Andriy complied with the order and cautiously made his way over to the guard. He bumped Fedir's side with his hip, grabbing his attention. His eyes indicated for him to stay nearby.

"I'm a soldier," Andriy explained to the man. He had moved his hands to place them on his head. "I came across this boy who was in danger." He nodded in Fedir's direction. "His parents had been killed outside of Shats'k. He was almost killed as well. I was bringing him to the border and then I will return to my unit," he assured the guard.

"Do you have identification?" The man was still suspicious, noting Andriy was not in military gear.

"I do. It's inside my right front pocket." Andriy offered his hip to the man. The guard rummaged through Andriy's pocket. Andriy said a silent, thankful prayer that he had put his identification in his shoe rather than the backpack that contained his research. He didn't need the guard any more distressed than he already was.

Pulling out the laminated documents, the guard inspected the information. He looked from Andriy to the record and back again. Squinting at the picture, he looked up at Andriy once more.

"Drop the boy at the tents and report back to me." He handed the identification to Andriy and waved them on through the gate.

Andriy grabbed Fedir's hand. "We don't have much time. I need a distraction." He searched frantically for a solution to the situation.

"What's wrong?" Fedir had been silent, following Andriy's direction without question up until this point.

"They know I'm military. I'm under a mandatory order to stay close. You heard the man; I'm supposed to drop you off at one of these tents and report back to him. If I don't, they'll come looking for me." Andriy had stopped and bent down to be face to face with the boy.

"I don't want you to leave me," Fedir's voice wavered, and tears began to well in his eyes.

"I'm not going to, Fedir. That's why I'm looking for a distraction. I don't want to leave you, but I also need to get to the President so I can report my findings. I've got to stop General Gorsky." Andriy tried to soothe the boy, but his own emotions were overcoming him too.

CHAPTER TWENTY-EIGHT

Boris guided the plane towards the landing strip near the Polish border. The airport had been hurriedly constructed in the previous war in order to get the needed supplies to the international convoys that had converged on the area to render aid. Over the last decade, the airport had been made a permanent fixture. Many upgrades had been constructed to make the airport a highly desirable landing area. Restaurants lined the interior bringing western cuisine to Poland. Novelty shops popped up to offer souvenirs for travelers. It even boasted a duty-free shop where passengers could obtain Polish bourbon and cigarettes. Now, it has returned to its original use.

Dawson noticed the lines of tents as they approached the airport. He wondered in which tent Stephanie was attending to the wounded and weary. His heart pounded in his chest at the anticipation of seeing her again. He wondered how he would begin the conversation. He wondered how she would respond. In the seemingly slow descent to the ground, being this close to her again, made Dawson realize he wanted to give the relationship another chance. That is, if Stephanie wanted it.

"Make sure that seatbelt is on. This isn't your usual commercial airplane landing." Boris' command woke Dawson from his trance. He fumbled with the seatbelt straps, finally clicking them into place. He watched as the ground grew closer and closer until at last, the plane touched down. The sensation of breaking was much more intense than what he was used to, but the plane eventually came to its taxiing pace.

Stopping the plane right outside the terminal, Dawson and Boris unclicked themselves from their seats. Dawson grabbed his paltry belongings and headed to the door.

"Hang on one minute," Boris announced. "I need to grab some papers for the airport security before we depart."

Boris made his way to the back of the plane. Dawson couldn't see what he was doing, and he wasn't paying him too much attention anyway. He started thinking about Stephanie again. He wondered if she had changed since helping with the war cause. *Would it soften or harden her*, he mused.

"Okay. Let's go." Boris walked towards Dawson. "Just turn that red handle, push out and then guide the door to the right."

Dawson opened the door. The airport crew had come to the plane and pushed the departure steps to the opening. Dawson stepped onto the first rung with Boris coming up behind him. Dawson didn't notice Boris tucking something in the belt loop of his pants behind him.

Once on the tarmac, Boris handed the airport security guard a manilla folder. The guard opened the folder, inspecting the documents inside. It was a signed order from President Bagan allowing Boris to land his plane in Poland. The papers further stated that Mr. Dawson Crane was his passenger and was here on a diplomatic mission to offer top secret information to the President. Discretion was paramount and the instructions stated that Boris was to take Mr. Crane to the Polish consulate immediately.

The guard finished reading the orders. He was suddenly alert and professional, as if his actions were being monitored. He handed the folder back to Boris. "Right this way, gentlemen."

"That won't be necessary," Boris offered. "Just give me the keys to a rental car and we'll be on our way."

"Of course, sir." The guard hurried to the guard post returning with the same speed at which he left. He handed Boris a set of keys and pointed to a green sedan parked just under a terminal causeway. Another plane was taxiing on the runway and the security guard quickly left to attend to the new flight.

Once the man was out of view, Boris reached behind his back producing a Makarov pistol. He shoved into the small of Dawson's back. "Move." Boris's tone was menacing. Taken off guard, Dawson tried to turn around to face Boris. He was met with further pressure from the gun.

"What's all this?" Dawson was confused. Boris was supposed to be helping him. *Could it be a ploy*, he thought.

"I have to kill you Mr. Crane," he stated plainly. "I either kill you or Gorsky kills me like he did my brother."

Shocked, Dawson started to shake in fear. "Sergei's dead?" He couldn't believe he was uttering the words.

"Yes. Sergei's dead, thanks to you," Boris spat.

"I don't know what you mean. He was helping me! I didn't contact him. He contacted me!" Dawson's voice was filled with hysteria.

"It doesn't matter. What matters is, he helped you. Oh, he thought he was saving the world. Well, the world doesn't work that way when someone else doesn't want it to be saved." He was guiding Dawson towards the end of the medical tents where an empty field lay. It looked to be some sort of landfill for discarded medical waste.

"Sergei thought he could outsmart General Gorsky. He was sorely mistaken. Gorsky has men everywhere. After he contacted you, Gorsky was alerted by one of his many moles that you had been contacted. The entire conversation was recorded. Gorsky knew about the passport and the disarmed tracking device. He knew you had a plane ticket to Germany under a false name. He guessed, correctly I see, that you intended to travel to Poland in hopes of connecting with someone named Koval."

Dawson's mind was racing. Gorsky knew about all this and still let him come this far. *Why?*

"I don't understand," Dawson said, trying to figure all this out. "Why would General Gorsky allow me to get this far?"

"So, I could live," Boris said absently. "When Gorsky found out that Sergei had started helping you, he gathered up our entire family, including my beloved nieces and brought us to the bunker where Sergei worked. He lined us all up. All but Sergei. One by one, Gorsky personally put a bullet in each of their heads. The children screamed as they watched their parents and family members die. Blood and brains spattered their innocent faces. It wasn't long before their screams were silenced. I was the last in the line. I prepared myself to die, but Gorsky grabbed my arm and took me away. He led me to a room where Sergei had been kept. I saw my brother. My baby brother was beaten so badly I wasn't even sure it was him." Boris shoved the gun harder into Dawson's back. His anger was evident. It was a bad sign for Dawson. Calm people rarely kill, it was the ones with a grudge that made a killer.

"Gorsky told me that it was my brother. I didn't want to believe him. My baby brother covered in blood, barely alive. Then, he handed me a gun. 'Prove your loyalty', he said to me. 'Kill your brother.' I begged the general to kill me instead. I was on my knees pleading to this man to take my life over my brother's. That's how much I loved my brother! Gorsky almost took me up on the offer. I could feel the cold steel of his pistol on my forehead. He didn't pull the trigger though. He told me to get up. I stood up, confused. I wasn't sure what the man was thinking. 'I need you alive', he told me. He turned his aim to my brother and fired two shots. One in his heart and one in his forehead. My brother died right before my eyes."

"I still don't understand. I don't understand," Dawson said repeatedly. "What don't you understand? For me to live, you have to die! Gorsky will have his way," he sneered.

Boris grabbed Dawson's shirt and shoved him in the direction of the field. Once at the edge, he pushed Dawson to his knees and put the pistol to the back of his head.

CHAPTER TWENTY-NINE

Andriy entered a tent closest to the edge of the rows. Zeus hesitated just behind him and sat down. He could sense something wasn't right. The stench of sickness sucked its way from the tent being opened. Andriy gagged as the smell entered his nostrils and he heaved from the nausea. Fedir covered his mouth and nose trying to block the odor. They looked around the frantic room. Nurses and doctors were racing between patient beds administering care where they could. A figure in a hazmat suit turned in their direction when the light from the outside radiated into the room. She finished bandaging a patient who had been stripped to the waist, blisters covering his chest and started walking towards them.

"Are you okay? Do you need a doctor?" she asked with concern, glancing from head to toe at the two figures in front of her. They certainly looked out of place.

Andriy was caught by her eyes. They were a hazel green like you see from the leaves in the fall right as they started to turn yellow. He could make out that she had blond hair. It was pulled back into what he assumed was a ponytail. Her voice was soft even from the distance she kept from them.

"Uh, no. We're fine. I think we're lost, actually," Andriy stuttered.

"Yeah. You don't look like you need to be in this tent. Hang on one second and let me get out of this suit. I'll see if I can't get you to the right place." She turned, leaving Andriy still stunned by her beauty, and made her way towards the back of the tent.

It wasn't very long before Andriy felt a tap on his shoulder. He gave a slight jump at the sudden distraction. Looking behind him, he stared into the same hazel eyes that had captured his prior attention.

"I'm sorry. I didn't mean to startle you." Her voice instantly set Andriy at ease.

"Oh, it's okay," Andriy stumbled over his words.

"So, if you don't need a doctor, what can I help you with? Do you need the food tent or somewhere to rest for a bit?" The nurse blushed as she tried to find a way to help the handsome man before her. She was just better at hiding her attraction, or so she thought.

Fedir tugged on the woman's shirt, drawing her out of her trance. "I'm hungry, and so is my dog."

The woman had totally ignored the boy and the dog. Bending down to Fedir's level, she apologetically looked him in his eyes.

"Yes. You must be hungry. I'm so sorry..." The pause was an opening for Fedir.

"Fedir," he stated. "I'm Fedir, and this is Zeus." He bent down and petted the dog.

"Well, hello Fedir and Zeus. My name is Stephanie." She smiled at the pair. "And what is your companion's name?" Her head turned to Andriy.

"Where are my manners?" Andriy said, embarrassed. "My name is Andriy. Fedir," he placed his hand on Fedir's head, "and I have been traveling for several days. He's right, we are hungry. Could you possibly show us where we might be able to get something to eat? I don't mean to disturb your work, so if you'd just point us in the right direction, we can find the chow hall ourselves."

At the mention of his name, Stephanie gave the man an odd look. The way he called the meal tent a chow hall struck a chord with her. Only the military called it a chow hall. The man before her had the physique of a soldier. He certainly was the right age for one too, but it was his name that caught her attention. *Didn't Dawson mention a man from Ukraine named Andriy that he was trying to get in contact with?*

She pushed the thought away. Andriy was a common enough name. She recalled a dozen or so soldiers that had come through the tents with the same name. He could simply be a young man that wasn't fit for military duty but always wanted to be a soldier. It happens all the time. Still, there was just something bugging her about him that she couldn't quite put her finger on.

She continued to stare at Andriy, trying to conjure an excuse not to tell him where the meal tent was in order to engage him further in conversation, when her gaze latched onto movement in the distance. Something just beyond the tent; closer to the airport runway. She could make out two figures walking towards the fields. She raised her hand to shade her eyes from the sun, hoping to get a better view.

She was able to start making out the two figures. Both were men. She could tell by their stature and the way they carried themselves. There wasn't anything feminine about them at all. The one walking behind the other was slightly taller than the man in front, but not by much. The way his shoulders were set, it looked as if he was determined to direct the man ahead of him into the fields. His steps were purposeful and focused. It was such an odd behavior. No one went into the fields unless it was to empty the trash.

Andriy noticed Stephanie's eyes shift to point behind him. He turned to see what had caught her attention. Immediately he noticed the two men. His eyes laser-focused on the man in the rear, his left hand steering the man in front of him. His right hand held a gun. He motioned Stephanie and Fedir back into the tent but stopped short. He didn't want to send them in with the sick patients only to be exposed to the infected unequipped. He searched for a place for them to hide.

Within no less than three seconds, he spotted a medical crate outside the tent.

"Get behind that crate." His voice was stern and there was no room for arguing. Sensing something terrible was about to happen, Stephanie grabbed Fedir by the arm and tugged him to the safety of the hiding place. Fedir did not question her actions for he also felt the urgency and danger about to unfold. Zeus followed the pair.

Andriy instinctively raised his rifle. Through the scope, he watched as the men approached the outskirts of the field. The magnification in the scope showed him immediately one of the men was his friend, Dawson. He didn't have time to think why he was here or what he had done to get himself in the predicament he was in. His military training exploded in his consciousness. He calculated the wind and distance to the men in nanoseconds. Through the scope's magnification he watched as the man raised his pistol to the back of his target's head. Andriy needed him to look his way, now!

"You picked the wrong gun for that!" he shouted.

Boris quickly turned his head in the direction of the bellow. He had been so focused on the mission of eliminating Crane, he didn't notice the man with the rifle pointed directly at him. He smirked at Andriy and turned his eyes back to Dawson.

The loud crack of a weapon was heard. There was a slight smell of hot gas, gunpowder, and metal as the bullet left the rifle for its target. Dawson had used the unexpected distraction as a chance to lean to his side in the hopes that Boris would have to re-aim his shot. He prayed that the little time for that to register in Boris' brain would be enough for the man with the rifle to take his shot. It worked.

Boris slumped with a thud. Dawson turned to see him lying next to him with a hole centered in his forehead. The smirk had been frozen on his face. Blood pooled from the back of his skull. Dawson scrambled to get away from its flow. He stood up. His legs weren't as sturdy as he'd like them to have been and he stumbled forward, landing on his hands and knees.

He heard the other man running towards him. The sound of his boots on the pavement was a welcomed relief. He didn't think he'd be able to stand on his own.

The man stood next to Dawson and held out a helping hand to lift him from the pavement. Dawson grabbed that man's hand and stood up, staring face to face with him. It took a fraction of a second for Dawson to recognize his rescuer.

"Andriy!"

"Dawson!"

They hugged one another as long-lost friends do after an extended period had passed. They chuckled with nervous laughter, still reeling from the events that had just unfolded. They peppered each other with questions.

"How did you get here?" Dawson got in the first one.

"I could ask the same of you," Andriy retorted. He still couldn't believe he had just saved Dawson's life.

The men started to fill each other in on the events that led them to where they were standing now. Both were oblivious to the trio that was making their way towards them and the guards.

CHAPTER THIRTY

Stephanie and Fedir jumped at the sound of gunfire. Zeus let out quick barks. They stayed crouched down behind the crate, unsure when to leave after the single shot was fired. Stephanie couldn't see anything. The crate was positioned in front of the tent blocking her view of Andriy and the men that were spotted to the side of the tent. She needed to see what had happened. Slowly, she stood up. Waving Fedir to stay in his place, she stepped from the shelter of the crate.

She tip-toed to the edge of the tent and peeked around the corner. Andriy wasn't where he had been when she had hurried Fedir into hiding. She let out a sigh of relief not seeing him dead on the ground. She turned her vision to the field. There she saw two men, laughing at one another. Another man was on the ground, unmoving. Dead, or so she thought.

Realizing that Andriy was alive, she went back and got Fedir and Zeus. They made their way to the two men. Their voices getting louder as they approached, Stephanie recognized them. At first, she couldn't believe what she was hearing. Her mind registered the man's voice.

It was Dawson! It couldn't be.

She knew he was coming to Poland, but she did not know he'd be almost killed before her eyes. She quickened her pace, Fedir falling in behind her.

"Dawson!" She shouted with joy and rushed to him.

Dawson turned just as she slammed into him, hugging him tightly. Dawson whirled Stephanie around in his arms. Happiness poured through him. He sat her down in front of him, looked her in her eyes and placed his lips on hers in a rush of emotions. They continued to kiss as Andriy looked away, pleasantly uncomfortable at the scene before him.

"Uh, hum," Andriy cleared his throat. His attraction for Stephanie melted away as he watched the couple. He had been unaware that they were an item. Andriy didn't recall Dawson mentioning Stephanie at the conference, but then again, the two had mainly spoken about work. He was a little embarrassed, but in his defense, he hadn't been in the presence of a female for quite some time.

Dawson and Stephanie pulled themselves apart and sheepishly looked at Andriy. Dawson was the first to speak.

"Andriy, I would like you to meet Stephanie. My girlfriend," he added with a hopeful glance at Stepanie.

A pink hue crept into Stephanie's cheek as she shook Andriy's hand again. Andriy couldn't tell whether the rush of color was due to embarrassment or from blushing.

"We've met." Taking Stephanie's hand, returning the greeting. His face lacked the flirtatious expression it had carried before in her presence.

"Oh, how's that?" Dawson inquired.

Stephanie swiftly filled Dawson in on their initial encounter. She explained that Andriy had just come to the tent with Fedir looking for something to eat when she noticed Dawson and Boris walking towards the field. Her eyes locked with Andriy's. She told him that Andriy shooed her and Fedir into hiding as he took down Boris. Admiration flowed from her mouth.

Dawson looked from Andriy to Stephanie. Something was there. Something he didn't want to admit. He always knew Stephanie was a flirt. She never acted on it when they were together. Somehow, he knew she had remained faithful the entire time they were together. Seeing the way she looked at Andriy now though, he wondered if he had been too presumptuous with labeling her as his girlfriend. Trying to sound unruffled by the exchange, he changed the subject.

"I hate to interrupt this reunion, but we need to figure out what to do with Boris here." Dawson pointed to the dead man.

"Who is he?" Andriy inquired.

"It's a long story that will need to wait until this mess is cleaned up. As it looks, we have company that will be wanting to know that answer as well." Dawson nodded in the direction of the quickly approaching guards.

Holding up his hands in sign of submission, Andriy approached the soldiers to explain. He recognized the security guard from the gate. He did not look too pleased that Andriy had not reported back to him. He and the rest of the group listened to Dawson explain why he was here, along with how Boris had come into the picture, and what role Andriy had played along the way. They listened intently as Dawson recounted the events that led up to his being here. The gate guard still looked at Andriy with suspicion, but he held his tongue.

After what seemed like an eternity, the guards seemed satisfied, especially after Stephanie had spoken for him, and allowed them to pass so they could resume their mission. Andriy was relieved. Fedir had been as patient as he could be. He finally tugged on Andriy's pants.

"Andriy, I'm really hungry," he pleaded. Guilt spread through Andriy. He had been so caught up in everything, he had completely forgotten about Fedir. He had quietly stayed out of everyone's way not uttering any fear. Andriy's heart broke that the boy had become accustomed to war so readily that he sensed when to keep quiet and follow along.

"I'm so sorry, Fedir." Andriy bent down and comforted him. "We'll get something to eat right now." He took Fedir's small hand in his own and they made their way to the food tent straightaway.

After their bellies were full and their bodies relaxed, Andriy noticed

Fedir's eyelids getting heavy. They had been in the food tent for some time, and it was all starting to catch up with everyone. They had talked about Dawson's neighbors that had been killed and his being tracked by the Russians. He also told them about Sergei's unexpected and welcomed help. His voice was heavy with remorse when he told them what Boris had been subjected to. Forced to choose to either kill his brother or be killed himself.

Andriy had filled everyone in on his adventures too and how Fedir and Zeus had come into his company. He told them of his analysis in the lab that led to his email to Dawson. All secrets, they determined, were allowed to be exposed and unclassified as they shared their knowledge of the chemical warfare they had uncovered. For them to find a solution, they each needed to know what the other knew.

"I'm going to have to ask your leave, I'm afraid." He cradled Fedir to his side. "This one needs some sleep. I need some sleep too," he added.

Stephanie stood up. "I'll show you where you can find a place to rest." She made her way over to Andriy.

"Hey. What about me? I'm sleepy too." A hint of jealousy in Dawson's tone.

"I'll be back in a minute to show you where you can crash." She sounded a little perturbed, Dawson noted.

It wasn't lost on Dawson the way her eyes flashed at him. He watched as she guided Andriy and Fedir from the tent, her hand placed casually on his shoulder. Dawson continued to stare long after the flap of the tent fell back into place.

Stephanie showed her companions to a tent among many that had been erected behind those of the medical tents. They were far enough away that the sounds permeating from the wounded barely reached those of the sleeping quarters. They were constructed with heavier coverings to also aid in noise reduction. The medical staff needed their quiet time away from the onslaught of constant cries of agony.

She had wanted Fedir to go to the children's tents, but Andriy insisted he stay with him. She softened at the protective instinct he had with the boy. She wondered if he had thought about what would happen to Fedir if he was sent back to war. She didn't want to ask. *Surely, he had had time to process all the possibilities,* she surmised.

"We're here. There are plenty of cots inside, complete with blankets and a pillow. You'll find a wash area as well, so you can clean up if you wish to." She opened the heavy flap of the tent. Andriy brushed against her as he peered inside the tent. The contact sent a shiver through her body. She stepped aside.

Clearing the emotion from her throat, she spoke, "Why don't you get Fedir settled. You can bring Zeus in too. We're fairly relaxed around here when it comes to people and their pets. So long as there isn't any fighting among the animals, they're allowed to stay with their owners."

Andriy still fluttered from the unexpected contact turned toward her. "Will you wait for me to get him settled? I feel I need to speak with you in private."

Stephanie lowered her eyes, afraid to show her interest. "Of course. Take your time."

It didn't take Andriy long to return. He let the tent flap fall as he made his way over to Stephanie. She had walked a few steps away from the tent. He found her looking up at the sky. It was filled with stars. Her breath caused puffs of steam as she exhaled in the chilly night air.

"I must apologize," Andriy started as he approached. "I didn't realize that you and Dawson were, how do you say, together."

"We're not." Stephanie turned and faced him. "I mean, we were at one time. In fact, we were together for a long time, but that was long ago." She was fumbling over her words.

"I'm confused," Andriy said. "When I saw you kiss, I only assumed you were a couple."

"Oh, that." Stephanie brushed away his concerned look. "We haven't seen each other since we split up. I came here to Poland to be with my friends and do some family research. That's when the war broke out. I wanted to help, so I came here." She waved her hand at the tents. She still hadn't answered Andriy's assumption.

"So, why did you kiss him?" Andriy needed to know. "I'm sorry. It's none of my business. Forgive me for my selfish intrusion." He knew he needed to back away from her, but he found himself hanging on to her every word, silently wanting her to deny her feelings for Dawson.

"Like I said, I hadn't seen him in quite some time. When I did see him, it was when you saw him too, on his knees with a gun pressed to his head. We had a history together. We lived together. I cared...*care* about him. I certainly didn't want to see him get shot! When I saw that he was safe, unhurt, my instinct was to run to him. I kissed him. It was familiar. It was a reaction to my relief. It was nothing more than a friendly kiss." Her amorous eyes contacted his. He didn't say a thing, he simply nodded, turned away, and walked into the tent.

Stephanie stared at the empty space Andriy had just occupied. *What the hell is wrong with me?* she thought. *A nice looking, uninjured man comes into camp, and I jump all over him like a bee to honey?* The war, the camp, and the breakup had all boiled down to this situation. Her emotions were all over the place. *This is ridiculous! Am I trying to make Dawson jealous to cover up my hurt? Am I trying to push him away, so it doesn't happen again?*

She still loved Dawson but was afraid to let him back into her life again. Could he make amends for all the times he made her feel alone in the relationship? Or was she simply scared by what she had seen over the past few days and realized how precious life is and didn't want to end up alone? Still troubled, she turned away and headed back to her own tent.

CHAPTER THIRTY-ONE

General Gorsky methodically strummed his bloodied fingers on the table, ignoring the pitiful moans of the man slumped limply in the chair behind him. His eyes bore into Tomlin and Alex as they seated themselves.

"What am I to do with you two?" he asked rhetorically, slightly out breath from his exertion.

"Sir," Tomlin started but Gorsky stopped him mid-sentence, raising his hand in protest at the pending excuse.

"Stop right there, Tomlin!" he commanded. "You've had every opportunity to capture Crane. He's a quirky analyst for Christ's sake. How could he possibly have evaded both of you?" he spat. "You had every resource at your fingertips, yet there he is, sitting on a plane headed for Germany."

"It's not that simple," Alex offered. "He had help," shifting blame to Sergei.

"He didn't have help at first. You were on his doorstep!" Gorsky stood up, towering over the men. "You had drones on his every move! You," flashing his anger at Alex, "a trained assassin, were duped by a pencil pusher!" He slammed his fist on the table.

"Guard!" he bellowed. At his command, the door immediately opened. "Take them to the holding cell." He walked towards the door and paused. "Bring in the brother." The general sat back down.

The guard hoisted Tomlin and Alex up from their seats. Alex began to make an attempt to fight the man off when he was suddenly nose-to-barrel, with a gun shoved in his face by another guard. He put his hands up in surrender and was escorted from the room.

As they were led away from the room, they were passed by another guard holding the arm of a man. He looked terrified. His shoulders heavy; eyes shifting back and forth at the sights around the room as if searching for an escape. *He won't find one*, Alex thought. His eye briefly caught Alex's, silently begging for help. Alex looked away in resignation. He was in need of saving himself, though he doubted anyone would come to his aid.

Colonel Stalin approached them as they reached the elevator. "How was your visit with the general?" His smug tone landed on Alex's ears like razors piercing his ear drums. Rage seethed within him. He desperately wanted to strike the colonel with his fist. He felt like a cornered animal and the only way out was to fight or die trying.

"Pleasant, as always," he said sarcastically.

"You disgust me." The colonel stood face to face with Alex. "All those years of training. Years of building you into the perfect soldier. The perfect assassin. All the tests you passed with flying colors. All those assignments were completed with precision and without emotion. To what end? A pitiful excuse? Blaming others for your failures? What a waste!" he sneered.

Alex lunged at the colonel only to be met with a punch in his stomach by one of the guards. He was ready to land another blow when a muffled gunshot rang out. The sound came from the conference room. The colonel's lips curled into a smirk at the sound, and he lifted Alex's head up to meet his gaze.

"You had better hope the brother gets to Crane before he spills his guts to the authorities in Ukraine." With that, the colonel shoved Alex away from him and made his way towards the conference room.

Alex and Tomlin were ushered into the elevator. The guard pressed the button labeled *B*. When the door opened, a wet, musty smell permeated the air. They were led from the elevator into what appeared to be a large cavern scooped out of the mountain. The space reminded Alex of ancient dungeons left over from medieval times. Doors made from metal bars lined pockets of cells carved into the walls. The floor was graveled earth, wet from the seeping mountain. Flood lights scattered their glow across the space. Alex had to adjust his vision to the meager illuminations. Apprehension cascaded its way through Alex's veins as the guard opened one of the cell doors. He shoved Alex inside and slammed the door shut. The key ominously locked him in.

Tomlin was put in a cell next to him. The lock clicked into place as the guards turned to leave.

"Hey!" Alex called out. "Can we get something to eat?"

The guards looked at each other and burst into laughter. Ignoring the question, they left the two men staring after them as the elevator doors closed.

Alex grabbed the bars and shook the door, hoping it would pop open. Anger, frustration, and fear welled up in him and he furiously continued shaking the bars. He let out a primal scream, piercing the eerie silence of their prison. The intense release of his pent-up emotions left him drained. He let go of the door and sat down, defeated on the cot inside the cell. He looked around at his surroundings. It was a basic cell. It housed a toilet without a lid, a sink that looked as if it hadn't been cleaned in a decade and the cot he was sitting on. He saw a tattered pillow at one end of the cot and a wool blanket with bits and pieces chewed from it, likely from the rats he knew gathered down here.

"Feel better now?" Tomlin's voice penetrated silence.

"Shut up, Tomlin!" Alex scowled. "You're just as much to blame for all this as I am."

"Maybe, but I'm not the one acting like a spoiled brat that didn't get his way. Where did you think you would get trying to muscle your way out of this situation? That was a stupid move."

Alex got up from his cot and pushed his face between the bars. "At least I tried. You stood there like a coward!"

"I'm not a coward, you idiot. I already have a plan in place to get out of this. Do you honestly think I didn't plan for this? Did you not think I would have a plan B? No wonder you failed. For all your so-called elite training, you're way too hot headed."

"I am not hot-headed!" Alex screamed.

Tomlin scoffed, "Of course, you're not."

Alex threw himself from the door and stomped over to the cot. He wanted to say more to Tomlin, but he couldn't calm down.

Tomlin continued in an unruffled tone, "Don't worry, kid. I'll get us out of this." He told Alex of his plan B. "Before we left, I notified the men I sent here in search of Koval. They had tracked him to a small hunting house when I called them off their pursuit."

Alex's mood immediately improved. He grasped a glimmer of hope. If Tomlin's men could get to Koval and Dawson before they had a chance to hand over their findings to the Ukrainian President, they just may get out of this situation. A small thought itched in the back of his head. He had been trained by the Russians. They didn't like mistakes even if they were eventually mitigated.

"They will either intercept Koval at the border, or they will make their way to the Consulate," he explained. "One way or the other, they will be stopped."

Alex said a silent prayer. His life depended on Tomlin's scheme.

CHAPTER THIRTY-TWO

Stephanie walked back to the nurse's tent, alone. Andriy had politely rejected her advances. To be honest, she didn't know how she felt about it. On the one hand, there had been an instant attraction to him when he first entered the medical tent. It seemed a lifetime ago since she first met him, even though it had only been hours. Part of her felt guilty too. She thought she still had feelings for Dawson. She was overwhelmed with joy when she saw him alive. *Was it joy at seeing him or was it from him not being killed*, she wondered.

When Dawson had called out of the blue to tell her that he was coming to Poland, she admitted there was a spark. She just couldn't tell if it was from genuine happiness or that she had been so lonely since she started working at the border, and someone with whom she was familiar was coming to her rescue.

She tossed and turned most of the night struggling with her emotions. Frustrated, she got out of bed way too early to start her shift and headed to the mess tent. There were a few people inside, mostly hospital staff getting ready to start their rounds. Doctors and nurses gathered at a few tables, talking quietly among themselves, drinking their coffee. They didn't pay her any attention as she made her way to the coffee station to pour herself a cup.

"I'm sorry, Steph." A man's gruff voice said behind her.

She turned to see Dawson standing there. He hadn't shaved and the stubble formed a dark shade along his cheeks. He looked as if he hadn't slept either. His eyes were red and puffy.

"Couldn't sleep, either?" she asked.

"No." He didn't offer anything further.

"Why don't you get some coffee and join me at that table." She pointed to a table in the corner, away from the others in the tent.

Stephanie made her way to the table as Dawson poured himself a cup of coffee and then joined her.

"Look, Steph. Um…," he started the conversation. "I'm sorry I've sprung all this on you. I'm truly sorry if I've put your life in chaos."

She snorted at his words, "My life was chaotic long before you showed up."

"That's not what I mean."

"I know. I know what you mean, Dawson. It's just all too much for me right now."

"I need to know, Steph. Do you still have feelings for me?" he asked; faintly hopeful.

"I don't know," she sighed. "I mean, when we broke up, we both agreed it was for the best. You'd go your way and I'd go mine. We agreed that we just weren't right for each other. You loved your work, and I didn't. These past few weeks have taught me how selfish I've been. Seeing families torn apart from this war. Seeing children orphaned. Seeing the elderly suffering, through no fault of their own. It made me think that the reasons I gave for leaving were pitiful compared to these people." She absently waved her hands at the invisible crowd.

"Don't say that, Stephanie. Whatever your reasons were, to you they were valid."

"How can I not?" She turned to him sharply before closing her eyes in exasperation. "I'm sorry. I'm tired. You want an answer. My answer is, I don't know."

"I noticed the way you looked at Andriy." Her eyes flashed at him at Andriy's mention.

"Come on, Steph." He opened his palms to her in astonishment. "I'm an analyst. I may have been too distracted by work to pick up on your cues of how our relationship was failing, but I can pick up on subtle eye contact between two people. Look, Andriy and I have some information we need to get to the President. I understand from the chatter around here, he's currently at the Consulate. Information that could make a change in this war. It needs to be presented together. Him and I. I have what I've found out and he has what he's uncovered. Together, we can show this information to President Bagan and, hopefully, he'll get President Wentworth on board too.

I guess what I'm saying is, we're both going to be in your company for a few days before we're able to leave. I don't see a need for you to come with us, but in the meantime, I just don't want you to feel awkward."

"Why weren't you affected by the mushrooms that killed Tom and Bob?" she suddenly asked, changing the subject.

"What do you mean?" Dawson hadn't thought about that. *Why didn't I die?* He ran over the mushrooms just as they had. He was sitting on his lawnmower when they exploded their spores into the air. He had been so caught up in staying alive that the question never entered his mind.

"Do you have a lab here, onsite?" he quickly asked.

"Not as good as the lab you work at, but it does come in handy from time to time when the doctors need to have blood work done," she offered. "It's the second tent from the start of the row."

Dawson stood up, took a big gulp of his coffee. "I need to get Andriy. We need to get to this lab." He rushed from the room leaving Stephanie dumbstruck. Now, she had something else to worry about.

Dawson raced to the housing tents, quietly calling Andriy's name into each of them before he heard him respond. "Dawson?"

"Andriy! Get up! We need to get to the lab!" His words were rushed but still whispered.

"Hang on. I'll be right there."

After a few minutes, Andriy appeared at the tent flap. He too hadn't shaved. Not that Dawson had given him any time to do so.

"What's the hurry?" he asked.

"Why didn't I die?" His question caught Andriy off guard.

"What? What do you mean, 'why didn't I die'? Didn't die when? What are you going on about?" Andriy was still trying to wake up from his slumber. He hadn't slept very well. His dreams were taunted with Stephanie's closeness only to be followed by Dawson's scornful looks.

"I didn't die when the mushrooms exploded. My neighbors did; I didn't. I was just as close to them as they were, yet here I stand. I don't have a mark or blister on me. Why?" He searched Andriy's face for the answer.

Andriy stood there for a moment, letting all that Dawson had said sink in. His mind started racing. His analytics research and Dawson's statement were like puzzle pieces trying frantically to fit together in the whirlwind space of mind. One missing piece that needed shaping came to the forefront of his thoughts.

"We need blood work." He looked at Dawson.

"I know. Stephanie said there's a lab here. Nothing high-tech or fancy, but we should be able to run some tests. Maybe they'll eliminate the knowns or show us something we're missing. Let's go!" he commanded.

Dawson and Andriy hurried to the make-shift lab tent. The medical staff inside turned their heads at the disturbance. The pair realized they were unknowns here and stepped forward to identify themselves. One particular man had been huddled over a microscope. Dawson approached him.

"Hi. You don't know me or my friend here, but we have some information that may help in figuring out what is causing the blisters on the soldiers and civilians that have been arriving here at the border." Perplexed, the man looked at Dawson.

"How do you know about the blisters?"

"Because I've seen them firsthand in the field and he lived through an attempt on his life in the United States," Andriy interjected.

"Look," Dawson implored the man. "I know it all sounds crazy, but we're both bioengineers. He ran some tests at his lab at Lutsk Laboratories, you've heard of that place, right?" The man nodded his head.

"Good." Dawson continued to explain what Andriy had uncovered and what he had found in his own research. As they tag-teamed their explanation, the man became more and more intrigued. After re-telling how Dawson had come about surviving what his unfortunate neighbors hadn't, the three decided that the first course of action would be to test Dawson's blood.

The blood draw didn't take long and soon Dawson's blood was being sifted through the analyzers. The typical readout showed his red blood cell level, white blood cell levels and various other elements standard in a complete blood count analysis. One reading level caught their attention.

"What's that?" The lab tech pointed to a spike in the chart.

"I'm not sure. It looks to be some sort of antibody," Andriy said.

Dawson racked his brain trying to figure out what the spike analysis showed. He hadn't been sick and hadn't taken any antibiotics recently. He hadn't received any recent vaccines either that would show a temporary antibody buildup. He put his hands to his temple massaging the answer from his brain.

"My spleen!" he shouted, startling his companions who had been deeply in thought. "When I was younger, I lost my spleen. I didn't take the proper precautions and did some pretty stupid stuff," he continued to explain.

"In college, I partied way too much." The two other men looked at each other, confused by what Dawson was saying. "I drank too much liquor," he explained. The men nodded at the clarification. "I developed a rare auto immune disease that no one could figure out a cure to. A doctor by the name of Davio Stenner was called in. He had done some experimental research on rats using mycelium. Mushroom spores to treat the same symptoms I was having. It worked!" Dawson was practically dancing in excitement around the men.

"That's what the spike is! Mycelium! I have antibodies to the chemicals that are causing all this."

"So, you're telling me that you have, within you, the antibodies needed to combat the chemical reaction that is killing these patients?" The lab-tech's eyes squinted, trying to articulate his thoughts.

"Yes!" Dawson said quickly.

"Then there's only one way to prove this theory so I can see for myself. We need to expose you to the blisters. It's quicker than trying to grow a culture in a petri dish, and we both know time is of the essence." With that the technician stood up and shook Dawson's hand. "I'm Petrov, by the way. I think you and I are going to become very close." He clicked his lips, leading Dawson out of the tent.

CHAPTER THIRTY-THREE

With Dawson and Petrov off to follow a hopeful theory that Dawson could possibly be the cure for all this, Andriy made his way to find Fedir and Zeus. He heard children laughing and headed towards the merriment. He spotted Fedir right away. He was showing the other children some of Zeus' tricks, drawing out squeals of amusement from his attentive crowd. Andriy smiled as he approached the scene.

"Are you enjoying yourself?" Andriy kiddingly asked Fedir, bringing himself near the boy. His voice was warm with affection.

"Andriy!" Fedir exclaimed excitedly. "Look what Zeus can do." He proceeded to give Zeus various commands, and the dog executed them without hesitation. It still boggled Andriy how Zeus had become such an integral part of his life. The dog and Fedir had become his family.

"That's great, Fedir!" Andriy praised. Fedir turned back to Zeus, continuing to entertain his newly found friends.

Andriy continued to watch the interactions of Zeus and Fedir. He reflected on his own family. His parents were getting up there in age. He had no siblings. He had no wife. In fact, he hadn't had a lot of free time for dating. He was asked during family gatherings when he was going to find someone and settle down. He always made excuses about work or some other distraction that prevented him from finding someone. He grew tired of the constant badgering. In truth, he wasn't sure he wanted to settle down. His brief military time had shown him the horrors of losing loved ones, and he wasn't convinced that he could endure it if he had been married now.

He also couldn't endure seeing Fedir orphaned. Alone in this war, finding his parents' dead bodies. What kind of trauma would the boy experience throughout his life? Would he suffer through hundreds of sessions with a psychologist trying to find a way to deal with his past. No child should have to live through such heartbreak. He wanted to shield his innocence from it all.

"Hey, Fedir." He motioned the boy to him.

"I'll be right back," Fedir called out to his companions as he hurried towards Andriy.

Fedir hugged Andriy when he reached him. Zeus padded his way over too, tail wagging as he strolled. Andriy gave a gentle squeeze before pulling away, a serious look cast across his face.

"Fedir, what do you want to do after the war? Or rather, what do you want to do now?" His tone indicated the importance of the question.

"What do you mean?" Fedir asked innocently. He found it difficult to look to the future. He was happy now, here with Andriy and Zeus. His eyes started to well up at the thought that Andriy was trying to get rid of him.

"Hey, now. What's wrong?" he asked tenderly.

"I don't want you to go," Fedir sobbed.

"I'm not going anywhere just yet. You know I need to help Dawson tell the President what's going on. You were there when I made my discoveries in the lab. I must inform someone of what I found. It will help with this war. But that's not what I'm talking about." he reassured him.

Fedir sniffled, "Then what do you mean?"

"I, uh, still want to know if you want to stay with me? Like, permanently." Andriy didn't know why he was suddenly anxious for Fedir's answer.

"Yes!" Fedir sprang up and wrapped his arms around Andriy's neck. "I want that very much. I haven't changed my mind."

Suddenly, he sat back down. His happiness instantly turned somber. "What about my aunts?"

"Tell you what, after we get through all this, we'll find your aunts and simply ask them." He tried to sound upbeat.

Andriy had forgotten about Fedir's extended family. He had no rights to the boy. Surely, they would want to take him in. He was blood. He was family. Andriy's heart began to ache at the thought of losing Fedir. He gathered Fedir into his embrace and held him.

"We'll figure something out, I promise." He kissed the top of Fedir's head.

Fedir clutched Andriy a little tighter. "They're going to send you back to the war, aren't they?" His voice was barely a whisper.

"I don't know. Maybe because I have all this information, they will at least let me deliver it to the authorities. My hope is the research will put a stop to this war and I won't have to go back. We'll just have to wait and see." He rocked Fedir back and forth in his arms.

Fedir's friends had grown impatient waiting for him. They called for him to rejoin them with Zeus. Reluctantly, he pulled himself from Andriy's embrace. He wanted to appear strong, but Andriy could tell the boy was torn. He echoed his lack of certainty.

"Go ahead. Go play with your friends. I'll think about this some more and maybe I can find a solution to it all," he said with false confidence. Fedir nodded his head and then returned to the others.

Andriy sat there watching Fedir interact with the children. They all seemed to share the same sense of community. He was certain that most of them had lost at least one parent either to the enemy or to soldiering. The children appeared resilient, outwardly unphased at their predicament. They pushed down their emotions for this moment of youthful camaraderie. Andriy secretly applauded them.

Absently petting Zeus and watching Fedir, he didn't notice the pair of black-clad men approaching the children or Zeus' sudden stiffness. They casually strolled towards them, raising no alarm. One quickly glanced at a photograph, then nodded to his partner. With one quick motion, one of them snatched Fedir, and the pair took off running.

A millisecond passed before Andriy comprehended what had just transpired. He sprang into action, pulling his pistol in front of him and gave chase. There were too many people around for him to aimlessly start shooting. The men ran faster than he could, and he was losing ground. He yelled for Fedir, gaining the attention of some of the crowd. They didn't understand what was going on until it was too late, and the men sped past them.

Andriy continued to scream. "Stop them!" His lungs burned as he tried to catch up to them. They were just too fast.

The men reached a waiting car. The back door had been opened for them to make an easy entrance into the back seat. Andriy heard Fedir scream his name as the door was slammed shut.

Andriy raised his gun to fire at the vehicle, stopping himself before he could get a shot off. His range was too far and at that distance, he ran the risk of hitting Fedir or Zeus who was in pursuit of the kidnappers. He fell to his knees as the car drove off, spinning its wheels in its escape.

Pain, horror, and anguish all combined, as Andriy opened his mouth in a loud piercing cry. Even Zeus couldn't maintain the pace of the car. Andriy caught up to Zeus and brought him back to camp where he hurriedly flung him into the arms of one of the nurses. He quickly turned and made his way to Dawson.

CHAPTER THIRTY-FOUR

"Dawson!" Andriy rushed into the tent. "They've taken Fedir!" he blurted out. His voice was coated in sheer panic as he tried to catch his breath.

"What do you mean?" Dawson asked astonishingly. He and Petrov had been preparing for Dawson's exposure to the patients. Petrov had covered himself in hazmat gear. Dawson had not. They were just about to leave the tent when Andriy burst in.

"They've taken Fedir! Two men. They just grabbed him and took him to a car. I don't know where they've taken him. I don't know how to get him back. Help me!" Andriy was distraught with fear and anger.

"It has to be Gorsky or his henchmen," Petrov said, adding to the conversation as he joined the two men.

"How would he know Fedir?" Andriy asked. His mind flashed back to the scene of the two men glancing at a photograph.

"Gorsky knows everything. He must have had some sort of inside intel. Given the information Dawson has told me, it looks like Gorsky is doing everything in his power to stop you two from getting to the consulate. If what we're speculating is true, his career and his approval ratings among his citizenry are at stake. That is not a position Gorsky wants to be in," Petrov explained.

"Do you know where they could have taken him?"

"Rumor has it, he has a secret military installation in Rycec, not too far from here. He probably is hiding out there. The Belarus people apparently still believe in him. His actions in this war aren't as popular in Russia as he had hoped. The people are tired of this hostility towards Ukraine. They want the peace they had been promised. The people, according to the whispers, are on the brink of revolt," Petrov elucidated.

"How can I get there?" Andriy needed to find Fedir. He didn't want to stand here listening to the grievances of the Russian people.

"There is a jeep just outside the tent. The keys are in the ignition. We keep it for emergency trips to the cities to replenish supplies. Anyone can use it as we never know when we'll need what. Drive along the border until you come to what appear to be the ruins of a mine. Don't be fooled by the emptiness, it has been converted into a sophisticated military installation. My father used to speak of it from the previous war. They must have brought it back to life. And it's well guarded."

"You gather all the information you need." He turned to Dawson. "Get my backpack from my tent. It contains all my research. Add it to yours along with whatever you find in these tests and get to the consulate. I'll meet you there if I can. Right now, I'm going after Fedir." With that, Andriy bolted from the tent.

Tomlin wasn't sure his plan worked until he heard the latch of his cell lock open. He had been sitting in the cold, damp cell, patiently waiting as he listened to Alex moan about their situation. He rolled his eyes as he listened to the man in the cell next door drone on and on about how their mission had failed and how he just knew that Gorsky was going to kill them both. He was about ready to tell the man to shut up when the door opened.

"Brian. Sam. Took you two long enough." Smirking, he stood up from his cot. He shook the men's hands as they entered, lightening the tension.

"Sorry, Sir. There was a little mix up at the border. The kids all looked alike; it was hard to find this one." He shoved Fedir forward.

"Ah, Fedir, is it?" Tomlin grabbed the boy under his chin, forcing his eyes to look at him.

Fedir weakly nodded his head, his body shaking with fear.

"Your friends have given me quite the trouble. Maybe with you here, I'll get things back under control." He pushed Fedir from him and to the cot.

"Lock him in here." Tomlin walked from the cell. He motioned for Sam to unlock Alex's door. "No one is to assist him, or they will be shot on site. Am I understood?" Brian and Sam nodded in unison.

Alex stood up and walked towards the door. He had heard the exchange and waited for his turn to be released.

"Not so fast, Alex," Tomlin warned. "You didn't hold up your end of the bargain. I wouldn't be here if you had done what you were supposed to do. Do you know how much I detest inadequacy in my men?"

"I told you before, it wasn't my fault. Gorsky hired the analyst. How was I to know he'd be a pacifist?" Alex sneered.

"Doesn't matter. Someone has to take the blame and it sure isn't going to be me." He nodded to Brian this time. Brian raised the pistol that had inconspicuously been hanging at his side, the silencer elongating the barrel. He raised his arm. With one quick *thud* of metal meeting flesh, Alex dropped to the floor. Blood oozed from the back of his head, gathering around his face before pooling outward. "I'll be sure to send Gorsky your regards." Tomlin shut the door to the cell and walked away.

As their footsteps faded, Fedir sat on the cot, tears streaming down his face. He had never felt so alone and scared as he did now. He had jumped when they killed the man in the next cell. He knew they'd kill him too. Or did they plan for him to starve to death? He curled up on the bed covering his ears, trying to block out the deafening silence of the cave. He didn't want to think about his future. He wanted to be returned to the time when his parents were still alive. When the three of them would gather for dinner or watch the television. He wanted to hug Andriy and Zeus again. He felt loved when in their presence too. Sobs overtook his tiny body.

Andriy had made it to the outskirts of the abandoned mine turned bunker not long after Fedir's kidnappers. Leaving the jeep and continuing on foot, he stealthily made his way towards the opening. The guards weren't protecting it very well. In fact, it looked to Andriy as if they were looking into the shafts at what was happening *inside* the bunker. Taking advantage of whatever was distracting the guards, Andriy made his way, undetected, inside almost stumbling over an old motorcycle.

Most of the bunker's occupants seemed to be in a state of panic caused by the general being there. They had heard the gunshots from the conference room. Everyone was on edge, scrambling for excuses to go home. The general had left the compound and Colonel Stalin had made his way to the communications room, leaving the analysts to stare at each other. One female was the first to get up from her cubicle and make her way out. With no one appearing to stop her, her companions soon followed. They paid no attention to Tomlin exiting or Andriy entering.

Andriy had to duck for cover when he saw Tomlin making his way from the elevator. He had never formally met the man, but Dawson's description of him fit the profile of the man walking flanked by two black-clad men. Andriy's blood had begun to boil when he spotted the two men. Impulsively, he wanted to shoot the men when he saw them but thought better of the idea. He'd concern himself with them later. Right now, he needed to get to Fedir. His best bet in finding him had to be the elevator.

He casually made his way to the elevator and stepped inside unnoticed. He pressed the button that would take him to the basement. The basement area was the only logical place to build a detention area. He hurried out of the elevator as the doors reopened once he reached his destination. He was surprised that the area had not been built-out. It was literally a cavernous area as if the building had been constructed over an old mine shaft.

His boots crunched on the wet gravel as he frantically searched the cells. He came across a man lying in a pool of blood, his eye blankly staring at the door. Andriy could still smell the faint odor of gunpowder. Fear raced through his veins.

At the next cell, he saw a small figure balled up, his hands clenched to his ears, methodically rocking back and forth. Andriy's heart skipped a beat. *Fedir!* He yanked on the door. The lock had been so rusted from the dampness; it easily gave way at his pull. Andriy rushed into the cell and touched Fedir's shoulder.

Between his crying and the babbling of the water streaming through the wall of the cavern, he didn't hear the door opening. He screamed out in fear when he felt the touch of a hand on his shoulders.

"Fedir. It's me." Andriy placed his hand gently across Fedir's mouth. His eyes told him to be quiet. Fedir instantly threw himself into Andriy's arms. He stayed quiet but his body shook with joy.

Andriy motioned for Fedir to follow him. He put a finger to his lips reminding the boy to remain silent. Cautiously, the two made their way to the elevator. Andriy knew this was a risky move, but he had no choice as this was the only way out.

When the elevator doors opened once again, Andriy peered out into the room. It was empty. He cautiously stepped out, waving Fedir behind him. Carefully, they made their way through the cubicle maze. Suddenly, they heard a noise behind them.

"Stop!" A command bellowed in the quiet of the room.

Andriy and Fedir immediately ducked and took cover. Andriy pointed to a file cabinet jutted out from under a desk with just enough room for Fedir to hide behind. Reluctantly, Fedir squeezed himself into the tiny space. Andriy brought his pistol in front of him and stood up.

Colonel Stalin was standing there; his gaze sweeping the room. By the time his eye found Andriy, it was too late. The last thing he saw was the brass projectile coming towards him at lightning speed. The crack of the gun shattering the silence.

As Andriy made his way back to Fedir, he heard the sound of a door slamming shut and hurried footsteps. Andriy turned to see General Gorsky and two bodyguards racing towards him. He aimlessly fired two shots trying to warn off the men. Mere seconds passed before they recovered from the ambush and started rushing towards Andriy again.

The cubicles offering much needed cover, Andriy backtracked to position himself behind the men. He stood up watching the confused men frantically search the area in which they had just seen their target. Andriy's anger boiled over again, and he aimed his weapon, firing off four shots. The two bodyguards dropped immediately. Gorsky watched them fall, his hands covering his head, tap dancing around the gunfire. He refocused his efforts and ran towards the exit.

Andriy, seething, re-aimed his gun. He let out a blood curdling howl as his finger pulled the trigger, emptying his magazine. All his pent-up anger released with each bullet fired. With blind rage spewing through the barrel of the gun, his aim fell short of its usual accuracy. He watched in disbelief as Gorsky, stopped for a moment by a bullet plunging into his shoulder, found his way out.

Andriy breathlessly lowered his weapon and made his way back to Fedir. "It's okay, now. They're all gone," Andriy reassured the boy. "We need to go. We need to get back to base." He held his hand out for him.

Fedir closed his eyes, let out the breath he had been holding, and made his way out from the cramped hiding place.

"Let's do this!" he told Andriy, mustering the wherewithal to take his hand. As quietly as they had entered the bunker, the two left, got into the jeep and headed back to the camp. Andriy's heart swelled with pride at Fedir's bravery. He also realized he was going to do everything in his power to keep Fedir as part of his family. He just prayed his aunts and uncles would agree. This was the family he longed for. Fedir and Zeus. He wasn't about to give them up.

CHAPTER THIRTY-FIVE

Andriy and Fedir returned to the base to find out that Dawson was being quarantined in a tent filled with blister victims; both dead and alive. He stared in uncertainty as Stephanie explained what was going on.

"They think that Dawson may have a natural immunity to the effects of the toxins found inside the blisters. The only way to tell undisputedly is to expose him to the patients." Her voice was strained with concern and worry.

"He could die!" Andriy exclaimed.

"Yes."

"Why would he have immunity?" he questioned.

"Because he's not dead. He was exposed to the toxins from the mushrooms in his yard at point blank impact. Then, he was exposed to his neighbors right after they were exposed. The neighbors died, he didn't. The only explanation is that he has some sort of natural immunity. The only way to prove it is to..." Her sentence faded as her face fell.

Andriy stepped in to comfort her. She felt good in his arms, but he was conflicted. Dawson had become a good friend even though they barely knew each other. He didn't want to cause a rift in their friendship. He also wasn't sure that having a relationship with Stephanie was a good thing at this time in his life. He wanted to do what he could to adopt Fedir. His desire to have the boy in his life overrode the desire for female companionship. Gently, he unfolded Stephanie from his arms and looked into her eyes.

"I'm not sure what's going on here." He cleared his throat from the emotions clogging his vocal cords. "I, uh, how do you say?" Fumbling for the right words, he continued. "I like you, Stephanie. I think there was a connection when I first saw you. Maybe it was from not having anyone to talk to other than a nine-year-old. Maybe it was from months being left to my own fortitude in a war. Maybe it was because your smile gave me comfort. Whatever the reason, the attraction was real."

"Was?" she interjected.

"Yes. Was." His face was soft but stern with conviction. "You are a nice person. You'd have to be to risk your life to help those here." He waved his hand indicating the medical tents. "This isn't your war. These aren't your countrymen and women, yet you came to help. That takes a certain type of courage. That's attractive to me. But I'm not in the right frame of mind to take on a relationship. And, not only that, but I also think there's still something between you and Dawson that you may not even realize."

"What do you mean?" she asked.

"I've seen the way he looks at you. I've just heard the anguish in your voice. There's a deep, underlying concern for his welfare. More than just a nurse worried about her patient. More than just an interest in finding out why he's immune. You care for him. Maybe the time apart has made you realize this. It could be seeing all this death and destruction has made you appreciate life a little more."

Stephanie didn't say anything for a few minutes. Her thoughts digested what Andriy was saying. *Maybe he was right.* When she saw, what she now knew, Dawson on his knees with a gun to his head, her world stopped. She had felt a sinking in her heart at the thought of losing him. When Andriy had killed Boris and Dawson was okay, her heart sprung back to life. She knew that was more than gratitude, it was love. She still loved

Dawson. And now, he was putting his life at risk again, exposing himself to the very disease that had killed so many of her patients.

Emotions welled up in her and she threw herself back into Andriy's arms. Not for emotional attraction, but for emotional support. She couldn't bear to lose Dawson. She wanted a life with him again. She wanted to tell him how much she truly loved him. She wanted to tell him how much she had grown up in these past few months away from him, especially since she had been here at the border.

"I can't lose him!" she blurted into Andriy's chest. "I can't lose him again."

Andriy comforted her like a brother. There was no allure of companionship. This was simply giving someone a space to heal from the uncertainty surrounding them.

It didn't take long for Petrov and Dawson to find out whether he was immune to the toxins. Dawson was either going to live or die upon exposure. Dawson had entered the tent of the patients in various stages of the disease with trepidation. His fear of dying shook his entire body as Petrov had guided him into the tent. The only saving grace he could think of was if he wasn't immune, he'd be very sick in about three minutes or even dead by midnight. Thoughts of writhing in agony raced through his mind along with the mental pictures of Bob and Tom lying dead on their front lawns. Snippets of him and Stephanie together played through the thoughts as well. He wondered if they were going to be able to be a couple again. He certainly hoped so. *Too late to dwell on that now*, he thought as he stood in the tent, shirtless, waiting for death to consume him.

Nothing happened. Petrov checked his watch. Dawson had been standing there for a full 20 minutes and nothing had happened. No blisters formed on his chest or neck. He didn't even have a red mark indicating that the blisters had started to form. His skin was as clear as it was when he first entered.

He turned to Petrov when he had told him that sufficient time had elapsed that would have shown at least some forming of the blisters. With giddy relief he reached to hug Petrov. Petrov stepped back, holding his hand up.

"Don't touch me." He was apologetic and alarmed at the same time. "You have been exposed, and even though you aren't showing any signs of the blisters, I don't trust this suit to have protection against direct contact," he nervously chuckled.

Dawson immediately stopped his approach. He had been so overjoyed at not being dead, he didn't realize that everyone was still very much afraid of the disease.

"I'm so sorry. But do you know what this means?" He practically jumped with joy. "We can use my blood to make antibodies. We can fight this!"

Petrov pumped his hands in front of Dawson, trying to slow him down. "Hang on there. We still need to do some blood draws and compare your system now to when you weren't exposed. To be safe, I want you to stay here for at least another two hours. If you still show no symptoms, we can assume you won't die."

After the agonizing allotted time, Dawson washed himself with the bio-cleanse solution in the decontamination shower. He scrubbed his body, still shaking with the extraordinary excitement of discovering his immunity. He was now grateful for the treatment he had undergone in college. The experimental drugs that Dr. Stenner had used to try finding a cure for his autoimmune disease. The drugs left him listless and distraught. There were times he had felt he was going insane. Dr. Stenner chalked it up to side effects and continued the treatment ignoring Dawson's protests. He had begged the doctor to stop. He didn't care if he died. He wanted to die. Anything to stop the constant hallucinations. Hallucinations where his flesh was being eaten from his bones by tiny mouths filled with oversized pointed teeth. Or the ones where his brain was exposed to hot pokers sticking their sharp points into various receptors.

The effects had been so real for Dawson. They caused him to lose even more weight than he had ever done before. By the time the treatments were completed, his frail body only weighed 101 pounds. He was so weak and puny; he just wanted to curl up and die like a no longer useful lab rat. Gradually, as his body began to adjust to its new immunity, Dawson's health improved. He started to gain weight. He felt stronger physically and mentally. Best of all, he was cured. The treatments worked.

As the water cascaded over his head, Dawson began to understand the correlation between their discovery and the cure of his mysterious autoimmune disease. His treatment had given him the antibodies necessary to combat the man-made toxins the Russians were using. They would be able to clone these antibodies and create a mechanism to either proactively vaccinate the population or eradicate the mushrooms through mass spraying of the targeted areas. It seemed the Russians were concentrating on military facilities or heavily populated cities where the most damage could be inflicted. If Ukraine didn't have enough fighting forces, then the country would have no choice but to surrender. This breakthrough could possibly end the war. It could also be Dawson's death sentence. If Gorsky could get to him before he could share this information with President Bagan, all this would be for nothing. Dawson wasn't about to let that happen.

Dawson met Petrov outside the decontamination tent. He had changed back into his regular clothes along with his lab coat.

"Ready to test your blood again?" he asked.

"Let's do this!" Dawson said enthusiastically. As they turned to head over to the lab, Dawson noticed Andriy and Stephanie in a seemingly intimate embrace. His heart sank to his feet. All his excitement at possibly finding a cure for the onslaught of dead soldiers and civilians rapidly left his body. It left him deflated and sorrowful. He had hoped that he and Stephanie could reconcile, but now that seemed impossible.

Andriy spied the two figures leaving the tent and recognized Dawson. He pulled himself from Stephanie and nodded in Dawson's direction. Stephanie's eyes lit up as she saw him, and together, they hurried towards the two men.

Stephanie threw her arms around Dawson's neck. Taken aback by this sudden embrace, Dawson looked at Stephanie, puzzled. Didn't he just see her hugging Andriy?

"I'm so glad you're alive!" she beamed.

Dawson didn't know what to say. He was full of mixed emotions. He treaded lightly in his response.

"So am I. It looks like I have immunity somehow. I don't know why, but I think it's from the treatment that Dr. Stenner gave me. We're going to test my blood again. If what we think it will show happens, then we need to present the results to President Bagan. Maybe his team can find a way to create an antibody for everyone else and put a stop to the mass casualties. Maybe even put a stop to Gorsky as well." He tried to remain calm and nonchalant, but deep inside, his heart was pounding in his chest at her closeness.

"That's wonderful!" Stephanie exclaimed. "What can we do to help?"

"While Petrov and I test my blood again, can you and Andriy find out where President Bagan is holed up?"

"You've got it, buddy," Andriy said, his eyes trying to convey to Dawson that he had no interest in Stephanie the way Dawson thought he had. He desperately wanted to explain this to Dawson but now was not the time.

The two pairs parted ways to complete their missions. Stephanie and Andriy first checked in on Fedir. The boy had put on a brave face after him and Andriy had returned to the base. Andriy had made sure Fedir was situated in their tent with Zeus before he left to find Stephanie and Dawson. Zeus jumped and licked Fedir as soon as the dog saw him enter the tent. It was as if he instinctively knew that Fedir needed his comfort. The dog had yet to misjudge any situation.

Andriy and Stephanie found Fedir and Zeus sound asleep on a cot. The pair looked so peaceful in their slumber. Zeus awoke immediately upon hearing the tent flap open but laid his head back down on Fedir's chest when he noticed Andriy. He silently wagged his tail as Andriy approached.

"You're such a good boy," Andriy whispered as he patted Zeus' head with appreciation. "You stay here and protect Fedir. I'll be back as soon as I can," he instructed the dog. Zeus seemed to understand this command by letting out a soft moan.

"Let's get some rest tonight. I think we all need it. I'll let Dawson know we need a break. I know he is super excited about his discovery, as I am, but to tell the truth, I'd rather wait for more time to elapse just to be safe that he won't show any symptoms. We'll head over to the command post in the morning," Andriy told Stephanie as they left the tent. "The field commander probably is our best bet at finding out where the president is. Let's just hope he trusts us enough to tell us." With that, Stephanie left the tent to find her bed.

Andriy turned to Fedir and sat down next to his bed. He wanted to spend a little bit of time with him before he found Dawson. He watched the gentle rise and fall of the boy's chest as he slumbered. Andriy gently rubbed the boy's head, feeling the coarseness of his hair on his fingertips. An indescribable love welled in his heart. Slowly, he got up, kissed Fedir's forehead, gave Zeus another *good boy* pat, and left to find Dawson.

CHAPTER THIRTY-SIX

The next morning, Dawson and Petrov found Colonel Wójcik's office. "Enter!" he barked when they knocked on the door. They found Stephanie and Andriy already in the colonel's office sitting opposite the man behind the desk. His stern look told them that he was having a hard time believing that the story they were telling him was indeed true.

"Forgive the intrusion, Colonel," Petrov said. "We have some information that we need to get to President Bagan."

"I gather you are to tell me exactly what these two have been trying to explain for the past twenty minutes," he said, nodding in the direction of the two sitting across from him.

"Yes, sir," Dawson began. "I know this all sounds preposterous. I find it hard to believe it myself.

"And who are you?" The colonel raised his eyebrows at Dawson.

"Oh, my name is Dawson Crane." He held out his hand to the colonel.

"American?" The colonel ignored Dawson's attempted introduction.

"Yes, sir." Dawson withdrew his hand. "It's a long story, and I'll be glad to tell you about it sometime, but right now, this is the information we have." Dawson held out the results of his recent testing. "This research shows I have an immunity to the toxins that are being released from the blisters found on your hospital patients. We believe that they were all infected by genetically altered mushrooms."

"Mushrooms?" the colonel asked incredulously. "You believe that the infliction that these patients we have seen are caused by some sort of, how do you Americans say?" He fumbled for the word, "Zombie mushrooms?"

"Yes, sir." Dawson knew it all sounded crazy. Hell, listening to the colonel trying to grasp that concept of what he was trying to say even sounded crazy to him.

"Please, sir," he continued. "Look at the results. Many years ago, I had a mysterious disease. I was knocking on death's door. The doctors had run out of ideas. Their only hope for saving me was to turn me over to a doctor who had been experimenting with the spores of mushrooms. His treatment gave me immunity to my autoimmune disease, saving me. This now altered antibody that I have makes me immune to the chemicals that have been systematically implanted in mushrooms. The Russians, we think, figured that if they could chemically alter an organic species, that no one could figure out how the people were dying. They used a banned chemical from the Second World War. A chemical so diabolical it had to be banned. It was supposed to have been destroyed. Apparently, it wasn't and General Gorsky got ahold of some. He then used drones during the cover of night to spray the mushrooms. When someone stepped on one or it naturally disintegrated, it released the toxins. Those who were immediately in the vicinity, died instantly. Those who were further away from the release had less effects, though they still had some. That's why some of the patients lived and some didn't."

"So, what does this all have to do with you?" Dawson's explanation now interested the colonel.

"Well, I was assigned to look into this strange occurrence after I received an email from Andriy." Dawson looked in his direction. "Andriy had discovered bodies in the streets with a strange patch of blisters. However, instead of these blisters being random and filled with a clear pus that blisters normally have, they were in clusters and filled with a brownish liquid. Andriy risked his life to get to his lab to run tests on the fluid. He relayed his results to me via email. We had met before at a convention," he added for clarity. "When I told my superiors what Andriy had found, they assigned me to work on its source. That's when my life became endangered. The Russians found out about my analysis and decided to use this chemical, we call it Zyclonmycolodide, ZMD, for short. It's a combination of Zyclon, the gas used in the prison camps throughout Nazi Germany to extinguish the Jewish population, and mycelium, the spores of mushrooms." Dawson stopped to catch his breath.

"And you are immune to this, ZMD? And the Russians tried to kill you? And you're here to help Ukraine? Is that what you're trying to make me believe?"

"Sir, I know it sounds insane," Dawson interjected. Colonel Wójcik held up his hand, stopping him mid-sentence. "I believe you."

Dawson let out a sigh of relief. His mouth was parched from all the talking and sheer nervousness.

"I am not surprised that General Gorsky would attempt something like this. Everyone knew of his façade when he took office. The Ukrainian and Poles wanted to believe he was better than his predecessor, but the way he conducted his coup let us all know that this very situation could arise again." The colonel rubbed his forehead disgusted that it didn't come to him as a surprise that Gorsky was behind all of this.

"What do you need?" the colonel asked his audience.

"We need to inform President Bagan of our findings. I don't think this is something we can tell him over the phone or relay in an email. It has to be done in person. "We need to know where he is," Andriy said urgently. "The longer we wait, the more Gorsky will have time to plan something else, maybe even more sinister than what he has done."

"Well, you're all in luck," the colonel said. "As it happens, President Bagan is not very far from here. He decided to stay near the border. On the Ukraine side, of course." The colonel didn't want anyone to think that

President Bagan was seeking shelter in Poland. "He has a remote bunker not far from here."

The four companions looked at each other in disbelief and thankfulness. They were prepared to put their lives at risk in order to turn over the information they had. But now, it seemed, they didn't need to tempt fate in doing so.

"There's something else you all should know," the colonel continued. The smiles around the room froze. All four of them turned to the colonel in unison, expecting the worst. They had become accustomed to meeting wall after wall, danger after danger to get this mystery solved. It wore like a broken-in glove, slipping effortlessly into their thoughts.

Steeling themselves against what the colonel was about to tell them, they faced him with determination.

"Not only is President Bagan very close, he's also been listening in on this conversation," he stated. "And for you, Mr. Crane and Miss Blevins, your President Wentworth is with him."

Stephanie and Dawson immediately looked at one another as smiles beamed across their faces. Stephanie held her hands to her mouth as she shakenly laughed into them. The entire room relaxed, and echoes of congratulations made their way around. They couldn't believe their luck. It was as if every fear, trepidation and danger lifted from their souls leaving their spirits soaring with relief.

Even though Dawson felt the weight of the world lift from his shoulders, he still jumped involuntarily at the knock at the door. The handle turned and in walked President Bagan and President Wentworth. Everyone in the room immediately stood up as the two dignitaries entered.

President Bagan made his way to the colonel. Standing at attention, the colonel snapped a salute to his president. "At ease," he commanded.

The Ukrainian president was dressed in combat fatigues. A picture Andriy had seen time and time again as he made his appearances on television, secluded in a secret bunker undetectable to the Russians. His constant appearance gave hope to the Ukrainian people and irritated

General Gorsky. It was as if the president was waving a red flag in front of a raging bull. His defiant demeanor and speeches rallied his troops into continuing the seemingly unwinnable fight. They also infuriated the general. President Bagan seemed to relish the general's frustration.

President Wentworth was also garbed in similar attire. The clothes were obviously made for a man, yet the lady wore them well. In trying to hide her feminism, the clothes only made her that more appealing. She was not only the first female president of the United States, but she was also the youngest, beating President Kennedy by six months in age. The entire county rallied around her youthful vision and thrived under her administration. She had such an aptitude for business and politics. World leaders hung on her every word as she spoke about a global community. The antics of General Gorsky were a thorn in her side and she was willing to do whatever it took to bring peace back to the nations striving for universal solidarity.

"Mr. Crane." She walked over to Dawson. "Your country is grateful for the sacrifices you have made. I cannot imagine the horrors you have been through to get you where you are today. I, too, am thankful for all that you have done to help eradicate this evil from our world. Your work, along with Mr. Koval has, undoubtedly, saved hundreds if not thousands of lives. I owe you a debt of gratitude."

Dawson blushed at her kind words and his heart swelled with pride. "Thank you, President Wentworth. I am happy to have been of service, however, this isn't over yet. We need to get an antibody developed and deployed to the people."

"We know. That's why we're here. It appears Mr. Tomlin was sloppy in his traitorous collaboration with General Gorsky. He left his findings on your work in his office. We had suspected he was involved with the mysterious deaths but hadn't been able to put the pieces together until now. There is a team of special agents hunting him down as we speak. He will be brought to justice; you have my word." She nodded her head slightly at Dawson and returned her attention to the colonel.

"Colonel." She looked at Wójcik. "We need to get Mr. Crane's samples to the labs in Washington as soon as possible. We have the best scientists in the world that can pinpoint the antibodies and clone them for use."

Wójcik seemed a little offended at her words and started to speak. President Bagan interrupted before the man could speak.

"I know what you're going to say, Colonel, but she's right. Not only does the United State have the most capable laboratories, but we also already have some of our finest scientists working in these labs. Mr. Crane's blood was the piece of the puzzle we were missing. We had the information from Tomlin's notes, but never put it together. Every scientist we had been working on this project had been scratching their heads trying to correlate the findings with the solution. Now we know. It won't be too long before we can end all this suffering and turn the tide on this war. You have my word on that, Colonel."

The Presidents' words comforted everyone in the room. It wasn't too long before Dawson was on his way back to the labs so they could draw several vials of blood to be flown to the United States. Petrov returned to his medical rounds, leaving Andriy and Stephanie alone. The two decided to get Fedir and grab something to eat while they waited for Dawson.

CHAPTER THIRTY-SEVEN

General Gorsky made his way out of the bunker. His shoulder screamed in pain from the gunshot wound, but he didn't give into it. He needed to find shelter. He needed to think. It would not be long before President Bagan would be informed of his involvement, no, his devious scheme to eradicate the Ukrainian population and secure his place as Dictator of Russia. He was dumbfounded at how quickly everything had fallen apart. He trusted the wrong people. It was too late for *what ifs*, he had to get out of the country. But first, he had to get this wound attended to.

The only vehicle he spotted was an old motorcycle. It looked like it had been left over from the cold war. Parts of the steel handlebars had begun to rust. The paint was a faded green that once had been used to camouflage the machine. Dirt coated the worn tires that looked like they should have been changed out years ago. Gorsky mounted the bike. The shocks squeaked as his body weighed down on their springs. A single key poked out of the ignition. Gorsky turned the key. The ancient beast sputtered and stalled out. He tried the key again. Begrudgingly, the engine came to life. Gorsky turned the gears on the handle, revving out old gas and smoke. Miraculously, it didn't stall again. Gorsky lifted the kickstand and engaged the gears. He rode off towards his second, secret bunker. If nothing else, Gorsky always had more than one back up plan.

It was a long, cold ride. He reached the duplicate bunker after about a half hour of riding. His face and his hands were frozen from the constant, chilling breeze. He hadn't been wearing a helmet for protection and his skin was numb from the exposure. The sounds of the bike alerted the bunker's security team, and they met him at the entrance. He got off the bike and strode towards them.

"General Gorsky." One soldier clicked his heels in attention. "We weren't expecting you."

"I wasn't planning on being here!" He snapped as he blasted past the man, holding his shoulder.

Once inside, he made his way to his office and threw open the emergency medical kit. He barked for one of the soldiers to come to his aide. "Get this patched up immediately!" he scowled, reaching for a bottle of vodka nestled inside his desk. The soldier gave him a thick wooden stick to bite down on after he had gulped down half the bottle of liquor. Soldiers were minimally trained in treating wounds. Those that wanted to go into the medical field continued their studies of the subject after basic combat training. This particular soldier lacked those skills.

Gorsky instructed the poor soldier on how to remove the bullet and sew up the wound between clenched teeth. Occasionally, the man didn't understand what the general had said and asked him to repeat the instructions. Gorsky grabbed the wood from his mouth, screamed the directions and replaced the mouthpiece. Eventually, the bullet had been extracted and the skin sewed back together, albeit haphazardly. Gorsky impatiently waved the man from his office after he finished dressing the wound. Gorsky collapsed further in his chair covered in sweat and blood, reeling in pain.

After an hour or so, the effects of the alcohol wore off and the pain started creeping its way back into his shoulder, Gorsky got up and went to look for some pain medication. He raised himself from the chair with his good arm. Dizzy from the loss of blood, he immediately sat back down until the wave passed. Slower this time, he got up out of his chair. Standing there, he looked around his office for another shirt. The soldier had had to cut the one he was wearing from him in order to get to the wound.

Finding a clean shirt in his closet, he worked on putting it on. He winced as he elevated his arm into the sleeve of the shirt. The pain was too excruciating for him to button his shirt alone. He walked out of his office to find someone to help him. He was met by a different kind of assistance as he passed out from the pain.

Gorsky was taken to a medical facility in order to recuperate from his wounds. He didn't like being here. It was not heavily guarded, the staff treated him indifferently, and the food was horrible. Something was going on with the staff. Had they somehow found out about his role in the invasion or even possibly his role in the altering of the mushrooms? Surely, his people would have intercepted any communications about it. Or would they also turn against him? He had to get out of this place before someone got to him. It was all falling apart right before his eyes. He wasn't staying around to face the consequences.

Less than 24 hours of being in this hellhole, he decided to leave. He got up from his bed and checked the bandages. At least the staff knew how to treat a wound. They also had got some blood into his system, so he wasn't so woozy. Trying not to show any weakness, he stood up and went to leave the building. When he opened the door, he was as shocked as the men who stood before him. They reacted quicker than he did.

Twenty-five United States Marines, dressed in black tactical gear greeted Gorsky as he opened the door. All color immediately drained from his face. Every man standing had their black clad M16s pointed directly at his chest. The useless soldiers guarding the building were kneeling on the ground with their hands behind their heads. Gorsky had no choice but to raise his hands over his head. He wondered how they found him. *They probably raided the bunker, and someone revealed my location.* His eyes narrowed as he thought it was either Tomlin or Alex. If it were one of them, he hoped it wasn't Alex. He had watched his progress through the years. Alex was a true comrade.

The team of Marines escorted Gorsky out of the medical building, snapping him back to reality. His men were rounded up and carted off in non-descript vans. Gorsky contemplated making an escape but the butt of the gun in his back made him think otherwise. He knew this was the end of his career. The end of his military power. The end of his life as he knew it.

He was taken to a military base just outside of Kiev. Ukrainian soldiers gathered at the base in droves, shouting with joy at his capture. As he was paraded before them being led to the prison, they raised their guns in unison shouting cheers of jubilation. Gorsky's capture meant the end of the war and they relished his downfall.

Long into the night, Gorsky lay in his guarded cell, listening to the celebrations outside. He remembered a time when the cheers were for him and his ousting of the previous regime. The cheers were still for his benefit, but not in the same way. These were cheers for his fall from grace. These were cheers for his demise. Because, he knew, his judgment would carry a sentence of death by firing squad. There wouldn't be a trail. He was guilty. There was no denying it. He also knew President Bagan would have ordered his death upon capture. This all was just a show for the people. They needed to see his capture for themselves.

He got up from his cot and walked over to the small, barred window in his cell. He was a tall man, but he still needed to lift himself up on his tiptoes to peer out the window. He could see soldiers gathered around steel trash fire pits, warming their hands. Their faces plastered in smiles, knowing that they were going home soon. Others clapped one another on their back, handing off bottles of beer. They tapped the bottle necks together before offering a toast and drinking the ale.

He longed to return to that time when they were celebrating him. He was still looking at the festivities when a man stood quietly on the other side of the cell. He raised his gun without so much of a whisper of sound and pulled the trigger. Gorsky fell instantly to the ground, his eyes still shining with tears of whimsical emotion. The man turned from the cell and walked away, returning to his compatriots in their triumphant merrymaking.

CHAPTER THIRTY-EIGHT

"Stephanie," Andriy began the conversation. Stephanie and he had found Fedir, and they all gathered at the table with trays full of food. Fedir wasn't paying attention to the adult conversation. He was more focused on training Zeus how to politely take the food he was being offered.

"I know what you're going to say, so let me stop you right there," she interrupted. "I know I came off as flirtatious and that you didn't know what to do or say. I'm not sure why I did it. I guess I was just lonely and still working out my feelings for Dawson. I don't want to confuse you or make you wonder where I'm going with all this, so I'll set the record straight right now. I'm still in love with Dawson," she said pointedly.

"And he's still in love with you," Andriy added. The look on Stephanie's face was that of surprise and confusion. Andriy continued, "I see it in the way he looks at you. I saw how he felt betrayed and hurt when he saw us together. He's a good man, Stephanie. I hope you can realize this."

"I do. This war has made me realize that he still cares, not only for me, but for all of us here. I just thought maybe I was confusing the emotion with the hero effect."

Andriy was puzzled by the term. "Hero effect?"

"Yeah, you know, when you get so caught up in someone being the hero and saving everyone, you want nothing other than to soak up their energy and those around him. It's like being drawn to a celebrity just because they are a celebrity," she explained.

"Ah, I see."

"But now I realize that's not my emotion at all. I truly missed him after I got here. I got so distracted helping everyone and, of course, being scared by all that I saw, I didn't have time to think about him. When I found out that it was him on his knees about to be killed, I realized how much I loved him." She sighed with the emotions of having to bear witness to Dawson's almost death.

"I'm happy for you that you found yourselves back to a place where you can start over. That's what I wanted to say to you. I've found that place too. Here. With Fedir and Zeus."

At the mention of their names, Fedir and Zeus both turned to Andriy. He put his arms around Fedir and drew him in for a hug.

"These two are my family now." He smiled at Fedir. "Since his parents are gone, I'm going to talk to his aunts and any uncles that may have not been volunteered to fight to see if they will allow me to adopt him. It's going to be a long road to recovery for our country once we can put an end to the General and his regime. It's going to take time and money. And, let's face it, Fedir's family doesn't need the financial burden." He whispered his last sentence so Fedir wouldn't overhear.

Stephanie looked at the boy, not with pity for his situation, but with the hope that he would have a better life than what he had been through in his short life.

"You're a good person, Andriy. We, Dawson and I, are so fortunate to have met you. I hope that after everything settles down, you can come visit us in the States and maybe we can come visit you as well."

"I would like that very much," he grinned.

"So, what happens now?" Stephanie asked.

"I would imagine with the information that we've presented to our presidents; they'll take that to the World Council for its decision."

The World Council was established a year after the previous war. It was created to replace NATO and the United Nations War Council. NATO had been unable to allow Ukraine to join due to the Russian threats of nuclear war thus tying the members' hands to aid the invaded country. The World Council allowed only those countries who had free and fair elections to join. There were rules against invading other countries without proof that a suspect country was doing something outside of a peaceful rule. Of course, a few countries balked at the idea of this newly created Council and started military exercises to puff up their chests in retaliation. They were quickly squashed by the sheer power of the Council and backed off.

The World Council would deal with Russia now that there was evidence of banned chemical warfare. They had been in the process of taking over the Russian government when Russia had invaded Ukraine again, but there wasn't enough evidence to do so. The General was very charismatic in his protest of the investigation and showed the Council doctored documents of Ukraine using the banned substance. Now that they had evidence to the contrary, Russia would have no choice but to pull its troops from the region. Russia would also have to pay for the rebuilding of the country. That cost would surely put a strain on its economy and its people would want to demand democracy. Russia would eventually fall into place and become a member of the Council.

"I bet General Gorsky isn't going to be very happy about that," she stated.

"I doubt General Gorsky will be seen in public after all this comes out in the open." Neither one knew the man was lying dead in his cell.

Lowering her voice, Stephanie asked the obvious, "Do you think anything will happen to him, like, will he be executed?"

"Probably." Andriy was emotionless in his answer. "It won't be from the Council, though. The Russian people, despite what the government posts on its state television, are not happy with the country's invasion of

Ukraine again. The last war was horrific, not only for the economy, but for families. They lost relatives on both sides. Remember, Ukraine and Russia are neighboring countries. There are strong family ties on both sides. It was like your Civil War, though it was more governments choosing sides rather than its citizens. No one wanted it then, no one wanted it now, but they were helpless to do anything about it for fear of government retaliation. In fact, and I know you didn't hear about this on any news sites in your country, people were beaten in the streets of Moscow if they were seen wearing any clothing in support of Ukraine or even having a conversation about it in public restaurants. Anyone caught filming arrests or brutality on their phones, was immediately taken into custody, and their phones destroyed. Most were never heard from again." He closed his eyes at the images running through his mind.

"How did you find out about it?" she inquired.

"Mainly word of mouth through the soldiers here. It happened to their family members living in Russia. It took time for it to be circulated around and get to the right people."

"That's horrible!"

"Unfortunately, that's war," he sighed.

Dawson entered the tent. All the excitement he had felt for having to have solved the mystery of his immunity to the toxins and the information that could possibly end this war was quickly replaced by sadness as he watched Andriy and Stephanie deep in conversation, heads close together. He had felt that he and Stephanie still had a spark.

Deflated, he joined the group at the table.

Stephanie's eyes lit up when she saw Dawson. "How did it go?"

"Everything appears to be in order. They took my blood and will send it to the labs in the States. Then, they should be able to develop antibodies to the toxin along with vaccines. I'm not sure how they intend to get them to the people, though."

"I think they can develop distribution sites rather quickly." Andriy joined the conversation. "Now that we know how the Russians were developing and deploying the toxins, they can contain the situation. I also imagine that since all this has come to light, there won't be any more toxins released. The mushrooms used as the vehicle to disperse the toxins will eventually die on their own. It would also help to get a message out through the public media, so the general population know what to look for. I'm not sure when that happens if the toxins would still be released, but at least we know there won't be any more growing."

"It was a senseless loss of lives, though," Dawson uttered. "It didn't have to be this way."

Fedir, who had been sitting quietly with Zeus, spoke up, "Andriy? Do you mind if Zeus and I go outside and play?"

"I'll tell you what. I'll join you." He nodded goodbye to the pair across from him and got up from his seat. He placed his and Fedir's empty food receptacles on the counter and left Stephane and Dawson to themselves.

"Stephanie."

"Dawson." Both tried to start the conversation.

"You go first," Dawson said. He needed to hear from her what her feelings for him were without any prodding on his part.

"I'm going to be honest with you." His heart dropped at her words. "I left our relationship because I wasn't ready for the commitment." Her words surprised him, but he let her finish. "I came here to Poland thinking I could forget our time together and immerse myself in my genealogy research. Then the war broke out and I immersed myself in that. I think I was running from my feelings and just finding anything that would exhaust me so much I wouldn't have to think about them."

She fumbled with the food on her tray, pushing bits and pieces here and there.

"When I saw you at the edge of the field," she continued, her voice noticeably shaking with the memory. "When I saw you, so many emotions flooded me. You could have been killed and I had been so childish thinking I wanted something you weren't capable of giving me. But what you were able to give me was exactly what I needed. I guess what I'm trying to say, and doing such a horrible job of it, is, can we try this again?" She was afraid of what he would say, and she kept her eyes lowered. She had just put her heart out there again, hoping this time, the man that sat across from her would want to start over, with her.

Dawson sat there for a moment, not sure what to say next. His heart was pounding so loudly in his chest, he was certain the entire tent could hear it. He could feel his face warming and knew his cheeks were turning red. Not with embarrassment, but sheer joy! She still wanted to be with him!

He reached across the table and took her hands in his. "Stephanie". She raised her eyes to look at him. "Ever since you left, I realized that I was to blame for you leaving. Wait." He stopped her as she shook her head and tried to interject. "You do deserve to have someone that isn't tied to his work all the time. I'm willing, no, ready to do that. Not only for you, but for me as well. If I've learned anything from all that I've been through these past few weeks, it's that I need to live life and not just exist for work. Sure, the work I do is important, but so is my happiness. My happiness is you."

Tears of delight fell from Stephanie's eyes. "I'm so glad you feel this way too." She got up and went over to Dawson's side of the table. They embraced, lovingly.

Pulling himself away for a moment, he looked into her eyes. "Just so you know, President Wentworth granted me anything I wanted for all my help. She specifically said that I could have a blank check. Of course, it's to be known that it didn't come from her directly, but she will be in contact with my boss. The only thing I told her I wanted was a month's vacation with you to any destination you desire."

Stephanie's face lit up with excitement and then she drew her lips close to his ear. "How about we get lost in the Amazon Forest?" she asked seductively.

"Sounds splendid to me."

CHAPTER THIRTY-NINE

Harold Tomlin thought he had made a clean escape. Days on the run had led him to a quiet, off-grid island in the Caribbean. No one had followed him. He was certain of that. The island wasn't on any maps, but he knew of its existence because he owned it. With the money Gorsky paid him, he found this little paradise and purchased it. He had originally bought it for a vacation spot. Its white, sandy beaches and tropical breezes was the perfect spot to relax from his job. No internet, no satellite radio; nothing but sun and silence for him to rejuvenate. Unfortunately, unbeknownst him, every move he made had left a virtual footprint.

It didn't take long for President Wentworth's team to find him. A wanted fugitive, especially an American one, didn't stand a chance. Deep in his subconscious he knew this day would eventually come, but he was still cocky enough to hope that it wouldn't. If he was being honest with himself, it really came as no surprise when he saw the four-manned military team walking across the beach towards him as he sat in his chair in the sand.

Part of him wanted to run knowing in doing so would cause the team to automatically open fire on him. Death would be instantaneous. It would probably be the best outcome knowing what he was about to be subject to. Basically, he was a coward when it came to his own life.

"Major Tomlin?" one soldier asked, confronting him with his weapon aimed at the sand, but his finger on the trigger.

"Yes," he simply said.

"You are under arrest for high crimes and treason against your country." He didn't read him his Miranda rights. Under military law, he didn't have to. Tomlin wouldn't be tried by a jury of his peers. He would be court-martialed and sent to the country's newest military prison. This wouldn't be a place where Tomlin could sit around and play checkers with his fellow inmates. No, this prison was comparable to the labor camps found in the remotest part of Siberia. The United States had learned that they had been too lenient on persons caught in the act of treason. Tomlin was going to be made the poster boy of traitors as a warning to anyone else who thought they could thwart the United States government.

Far above the tiny island, a plane heading towards South America flew over. Dawson and Stephanie were cozied up to one another, their thoughts on their Amazon adventure. They knew nothing, nor cared, about the man thousands of feet below them being hand-cuffed and led away to his final punishment.

On the other side of the world, Andriy and Fedir, followed closely by Zeus, walked up the stairs of a porch. Nervously, Andriy knocked on the door. A small lady opened the door. Her eyes lit up at the sight of Fedir. She squealed with delight at the sight of her nephew and wrapped him in her arms, rocking back and forth with happiness.

"Mrs. Dolesky?" Andriy cleared his throat anxious to get this ordeal sorted out. He didn't know what the outcome of this conversation would be. He had wanted to take Fedir and set up a life with him without contacting any family members. He knew that wasn't the right thing to do, but he dreaded the thought of not ever being able to see Fedir again.

He wanted so badly to adopt him. After finding Fedir's aunt, he decided to take his chances. Even if Fedir's family didn't want him to adopt the boy, maybe they would make him an honorary uncle.

"My name is Andriy Koval. I was the one who found Fedir after his parents were killed. Do you mind if I come inside? I'd like to talk to you about Fedir's future."

CHAPTER FORTY

It was a mildly warm summer day. Dawson was flipping burgers at the grill. His eyes concentrated on the meat making sure they didn't get too much cooking on each side. He looked over to see Stephanie pick up a small girl who had been picking flowers from the flower garden near the back of the house. Her yellow summer dress blew effortlessly as she was whisked away by the tall blonde woman. She giggled happily as the woman swung her around. He couldn't believe how much he loved that little girl.

Two years had passed since the Ukrainian war had ended. Once the United States found out that Russia had been trying to use chemical warfare on the Ukrainian citizens, it didn't take long for the regime to be destroyed. With the government embarrassed on the world stage, it had reluctantly decided to hold democratic elections. It was a change many Russian citizens embraced. For far too long they had been dictated to and now, they finally had a say in the way that things would be run.

The nightmares from what he had gone through slowly subsided, but every now and then, he would wake up in the middle of the night, sweating. Stephanie would comfort him and hold him until the nightmare passed.

Dawson had gotten up the nerve to ask Stephanie to marry him when they got back from their month-long Amazon jungle trip. She readily said yes.

"Mommy!" She laughed, handing Stephanie a small bouquet of flowers she had just picked. "Look what I picked for you!"

Stephanie took the flowers from the girl, giving her a kiss on the cheek. "Thank you, sweetheart. Let's go show Daddy."

Stephanie took the girl's hand and they walked, practically skipping, towards Dawson, laughing and smiling in a moment of sheer happiness. His eyes filled with tears of joy as he watched his wife and daughter skip their way over to him.

As he was watching them approach, he saw a silver car pull into the driveway. He waved his hand in salutation in its direction. A familiar man got out of the car and waved back. The passenger door opened, and a boy got out followed by a small brown dog. Not bothering to shut the door, he ran towards Dawson in excitement.

"Uncle Dawson!" he shouted as he hurried along, stopping only momentarily to give the girl a hug. Fedir plowed into Dawson's arms, embracing him with a warm hello.

"You're looking good, Andriy," Dawson said, shaking the visitor's hand after breaking away from Fedir's hug, but not before he gave him a warm hug back and gave Zeus a quick scratch under his chin.

"And you too, my friend. I see Olivia is growing. My! It's only been six months since I last saw you and she must have grown six inches!"

"Fedir has been doing some growing of his own," Dawson replied, tussling the boy's full head of hair. "It's good to see you, my friend. And Fedir, too."

"Do you have a moment to talk?" Andriy whispered to Dawson, his brow furrowed in seriousness.

By the look of his friend's face, Dawson knew something was wrong. He politely excused himself from the kids, kissed Stephanie on the cheek, quietly speaking in her ear, "I'll be right back." He led Andriy to the side of the house where their conversation couldn't be overheard. "What's wrong Andriy?"

Andriy placed his hand on Dawson's shoulder. His voice was hesitant. Taking a deep breath, he spoke. "Remember that souvenir you picked up for me when you and Stephanie were on your trip? The one you said was some ancient artifact?"

"Yeah, the store clerk had hundreds of them. He claimed they were from some ancient Mayan tribe that traded along the Amazon River. He was so serious about the trinkets in his shop; trying to persuade tourists that they could own a piece of treasure. I thought it was all for show. Why? What did you find?"

"You're not going to believe this. I didn't want to talk over the phone or put it in an email. What you gave me *actually is* an ancient Mayan piece. In fact, it belonged to K'inich Janaab Pakal, better known as Pakal the Great."

"Okay. So, it's valuable, so what," Dawson shrugged. "How much are we talking about? What's it worth?"

"Oh, it's priceless. But that's not the point. The reason this particular piece is so important is that not only did it belong to Pakal the Great, but it's also said to have youthful properties. Many people have been looking for a piece like this for hundreds of years. This particular piece is part of a treasure that is worth more gold than your country has stored in Fort Knox! And someone has been alerted to its existence and that you have found it."

"How do you know all this?" Dawson was shocked by Andriy's revelation.

"Because I found this inside the cardboard of the box you sent it in. I had packed it away when Fedir's aunt agreed to the adoption. I needed a new place for the two of us, so I didn't take it out of the box until recently. "Andriy held out a tiny, black dot. Upon further inspection, Dawson could see that it was a disabled tracking device.

"Not again!" Dawson's heart started to sink. He looked in horror at Andriy.

Andriy simply smiled. "Ready for another adventure?"

ABOUT THE AUTHOR

PT Bateman is a thrilling suspense writer residing in the picturesque state of Maryland, USA, where she shares her home with her four beloved rescue pets. From a young age, PT Bateman harbored an insatiable passion for storytelling and the written word, which eventually led her down the enthralling path of becoming a suspense novelist.

While writing remains her true passion, PT Bateman is also a full-time employee, proving that determination and perseverance are the keys to unlocking one's dreams. Despite the challenges of a busy professional life, she never loses sight of her commitment to her readers and the art of suspenseful storytelling.

Outside of her literary pursuits, PT Bateman finds solace and joy in the wonders of gardening. Tending to her plants and flowers, she nurtures a connection with nature that mirrors the growth and evolution of her own characters. Additionally, her love for books extends beyond reading, as she takes pleasure in various book-related crafts, breathing life into her stories even beyond the confines of the written word.

Stay tuned for more heart-stopping adventures from PT Bateman, as she continues to push the boundaries of suspense fiction and leave an indelible mark on the literary landscape.